AF415875

THE ALIEN'S SHEPHERD

USA TODAY BESTSELLING AUTHORS

ARIZONA TAPE
SKYE MACKINNON

Copyright © 2023 Arizona Tape and Skye MacKinnon

http://www.skyemackinnon.com

http://arizonatape.com

Cover by Peryton Covers.

Formatting by Peryton Press.

All Rights Reserved.

Please don't pirate this book. We really wouldn't want you to get abducted by evil aliens who specialise in dealing with pirates.

This is a work of fiction. Names, characters, places, and incidents either are the products of the author's imagination or are used fictitiously. Any resemblance to actual persons, living or dead, businesses, companies, events, or locales is entirely coincidental.

To our readers, who've followed us through time and space.

CONTENTS

[1]

HEATHER

The herd of white sheep looked comical on the purple grass of Kyven. It was clear they didn't belong here but they didn't seem to care, and instead were eating as much as their greedy stomachs allowed.

I weaved my way through the sea of wool on legs and patted a few soft heads on my way through. Cloudling let out a soft bleat and I gave her an extra scratch between her ears. "I know, it's a lot to get used to, isn't it? New home, new planet, new food."

As if she understood, Cloudling bleated again and ate a pluck of long purple grass, chewing on it leisurely.

"You seem to be adjusting well." I ran my hands through her soft fur, picking out some thorny material from the nearby bushes that could leave nasty marks. "You're doing better than me, then."

A light chuckle came from behind me. "I see you're still talking to the sheep, Heather."

I turned and raised my arm to greet my cousin. "Hey! And you can't say much, you talk to the Highland cows."

"Yes, but they're so much smarter, they actually know what I'm saying," Rachel said with a grin.

"Agree to disagree." I patted Cloudling's head. "Don't you listen to her. I know you're very clever."

She gave me a vacant stare.

"Never mind." With another scratch, I turned back to Rachel. "What are you doing here?"

"Just came to check on you. You've been spending a lot of time out in the pasture." She gave me a concerned look. "Is everything okay?"

We wandered down the grassy hill, back to the farm. "Yes, everything is alright."

"You sure? You're not regretting moving to Kyven?"

"Well, we didn't have much choice. The bank was about to take everything away from us." I gestured around the foreign landscape. "And this was our only option apart from going bankrupt and losing everything we'd worked hard for. Don't worry about me, I'm fine. Kyven is great."

"And you don't miss Earth?"

"I miss certain things about it. The smell of fresh hay, my breakfast cereal, and cheese."

"We have cheese," Rachel pointed out as she held the door of the farm house open, grimacing. "Although

I'll admit that Highland cow milk isn't exactly producing the best kind of cheese."

"Yes and it's very tedious to make. I miss supermarkets. Yoghurt, milk in my tea, parmesan cheese, cream donuts. Oh, cheese strings."

My cousin laughed. "Well, I'm glad you said that because I have a favour to ask."

"Oh no, I know that tone. What is it?"

"So, I talked to the Ta-Kavalla sisters and they seem in need of more supplies for their animal park. And I checked our inventory and we're running low on feed for the cows."

"There's plenty of grass," I pointed out.

"Yes, but the Highlands are a little more picky than your sheep. Anyway, they're arranging a trip down to Earth and they wanted to know if you and I wanted to go as well."

I put the kettle on the stove. "So what's the favour?"

"I kind of want to stay with Tamsia. She's amazing but she has horrid taste in interior design, so I want to keep an eye on her while we're in the middle of building our house."

"You want me to go on my own?"

Rachel folded her hands together. "Please? I'll owe you."

"You already owe me from that week I scooped waste by myself, do you remember?" That had been back on Earth. It felt like a lifetime ago.

"My wrist was sprained and I paid you back by

taking Lorrie to the vet. You know how feisty that chicken was? She scratched both my arms."

"I lied to my parents about who drew smileys on the barn."

Rachel rolled her eyes. "I was six!"

"Fine. I'll go. I'm bored anyway and I could do with a new adventure."

"Bored?" Rachel gave me a befuddled look. "We got beamed up on a spaceship and we're on an alien planet with purple grass and the most amazing animals ever. How can you be bored?"

"I don't know. It's a different planet but it's just the same-old life, just without money worries and stresses from the bank. It's boring." I finished making tea and handed Rachel one of the mugs. "So tell me more details about the trip. When is it? Who else is going?"

"Sahra and Abby. They're visiting her parents."

"Right, she's the only one who didn't disappear mysteriously. Oh, do I need a fake identity? The last thing I want is to get in trouble with the bank. I can't imagine they're happy with us running from our mortgage."

Rachel took a sip from her tea and pushed the mug away with a disappointed grimace. "Tastes rubbish. And you'd have to ask how Tilly does it whenever she visits. She's still being wanted for the disappearance of all the zoo animals."

"When is the trip?"

"Next week. A Kyven week, I mean. They've struck a deal with an old friend of Valla to make a detour to Earth. Someone called Ellabeth? She's the captain of the ship."

It was tempting. Rachel was right, living on an alien planet was supposed to be exciting, but we'd been on Kyven for several months and I'd got used to the monotony of looking after the sheep. My cousin had her mate, just like the other two humans living nearby. I was the odd one out. Rachel tried her best to spend time with me, but I still felt like a fifth wheel all the time. Hence why I spent so much time with the sheep.

Going to Earth would be a good break from my routine. It was kind of exciting to return. Back when Rachel and I had lived at our farm, I'd always dreamed of travelling the world. I'd wanted adventures. Being abducted by aliens - well, kind of - definitely counted as an adventure, but by now that excitement had waned. Coming up with a fake identity and hoping I wouldn't be recognised sounded like fun. Just the adrenaline kick I was looking for.

"Alright," I said with a dramatic sigh. "I'll do it. But you owe me a favour. A big one."

Rachel threw her arms around me and hugged me tight. "Thank you, Heather! I promise I'll look after the sheep while you're gone. I might even teach them some tricks. If they are as intelligent as you say."

[2]

ATINA

The intercom chimed and the red lights on my dashboard flashed in warning.

"Preparing to land," I said, reaching up for a switch. "Switching off the main boosters in five, you ready?

My headset crackled with Katak's deep voice. "Heard, I'm ready to stabilise. Ready in five, four, three—"

"Two. One," I finished the count as I killed the boosters. A tremor coursed through the shuttle before the stabilisers kicked in. Even though I'd done this easily hundreds of times, there was always a thrill when it went right and our ship didn't crash down.

I checked the camera to make sure our landing dock was free and clear. It was getting dark so I pressed a button to put some of the bigger lights on for a better, guided view. Some pilots considered those the training wheels of landing a ship but I preferred delivering my passengers safely.

As we neared the ground, another voice came through my headset. "Atina, status update."

"Touchdown imminent in twenty ticks, Captain," I replied, guiding the shuttle into its bay.

A set of orange lights flicked on and I danced my fingers over the control panel, calling a status report to figure out what was setting off the alarm. A long list of potential bugs rolled up the screen but none of them jumped out at me as a real issue.

Katak's voice came through my headset again. "Ready to deploy legs on your cue, Atina."

I checked the metre to check how far we still had left to go. "Deploy in two ticks. I'll set the count."

"Understood."

I allowed the ship to descend a little more before I reached up for another switch. "Deploy landing legs in five, four, three, two, one."

"Legs are out," Katak informed.

"Great. I'm going to turn off the secondary boosters, is the stabiliser holding?"

"It's holding."

"Good. Turning off the boosters. Prepare for touchdown in five, four, three—" A shock wave travelled through the ship as we made contact. I could feel the ship practically groan in protest and multiple lights pinged on around me.

The captain's low voice screeched through my headset. "What was that?"

"Sorry, Cap. Must have misjudged our distance to the ground but we're all set."

"Do better next time."

"Yes, Captain." I called for another status report again, relieved when nothing seemed to be on fire or damaged. Repairs were expensive and I really couldn't afford another deduction from my paycheck.

I released myself from my chair and stretched the strain from my muscles, glad that we'd arrived. As much fun as it was to fly and zap through space, there was something to be said for home sweet home.

On my way out, I ran into Katak coming out of the other cockpit, stretching his long arms. He stopped once he saw me. "What happened?"

"I must've misjudged the count."

"Really?" He seemed surprised. "You never misjudge."

"There's a first time for everything."

We made our way down to the exit hatch and I hopped down instead of using the ramp. It was more fun that way.

My boots thudded hard on the metal surface and the spicy sweet scent of Kyven greeted me over the smell of oil, gas, and grease. There really was no place like home. It was a shame we weren't sticking around longer. From the morning briefing, I'd gathered we'd only restock and pick up some passengers before we went on our merry way again.

There wouldn't be enough time to visit my brother or my two aunties, who always kept a jar of sweets ready for my brief visits. Hopefully I'd at least get the chance to buy some snacks at the terminal's shop.

This spaceport was fairly small for Kyven standards, but at least it had a shop full of local delicacies. It was mostly aimed at tourists, but with no time to drive into the closest town, I had no choice but to get some overpriced goods there. Maybe I should get the captain a treat to apologise for the bumpy landing. I still didn't quite know what had happened. I was a good pilot, no, I had to have more self-confidence. I was the best. It was why Ellabee had hired me and had even paid me a bonus to sign with her crew. Maybe the shuttle was getting old. I should have one of the engineer chicks on the PoTA-2 check it out.

While Katak supervised the loading of supplies, I went shopping. Near the spaceport's exit, a holo poster caught my attention. A new animal park with alien beasts was advertising that they were only twenty clicks from the terminal. Maybe I could visit them next time, if we had more time on Kyven. I also had my next shore leave coming up soon. Two whole weeks to spend planetside. I had no idea what to do with all that time besides getting spoiled by my aunties and annoying my brother.

Deep in thought, I automatically pointed at things in the virtual shop display. My favourite snack bars were out of stock, making me even grumpier than I already felt. Everything was going wrong today. I wouldn't be surprised if the day continued like that. I didn't know anything about the passengers we were supposed to pick up, but I bet they were going to turn out to be spoiled brats like the last people we'd had on the PoTA-2. I understood that Ellabee was making good money by renting out two of the cabins to paying guests, but why did they always have to be boring, rude or pompous?

I decided I didn't want to meet today's passengers, so I finished my shopping as fast as possible. The display told me that my purchases would be delivered to the shuttle five ticks before takeoff. Close, but if we got delayed by a bit, I'd be able to make up for that on the flight to the PoTA-2. Captain Ellabee would understand once I handed her the clovian biscuit I'd ordered for her.

Back on the shuttle, I turned on the outside cameras to watch for our passengers. The manifest said to expect three of them, all females, one Kyven and two humans, whatever that was. Katak was finishing up the loading of the shuttle, slaving away while I put up my feet on the console in front of me. Living the pilot life. I grimaced and switched to a different camera angle. There they were, our three passengers, making their way through the hangar. They were on time, which didn't bode well for my last-minute shop delivery. Now I couldn't blame any delay on them.

I turned on the boarding lights which illuminated their path onto the shuttle. The Kyven walked confidently up the ramp; she'd clearly travelled by shuttle and space ship before. Holding the Kyven's hand was a brown-haired female who was laughing at something her companion had said. But who really drew my attention was the pale female behind them. She was more hesitant, looking at everything with wide eyes. She was a kyvenoid with two arms and two legs, but she was a little smaller than the average Kyven female. The top of her ears were rounded, which made it look a little as if someone had shaved off her pointy tips. Hopefully she was born this way and it was not the effect of an accident or worse. The human also lacked throat filters, but that was fairly standard for other alien species. Most aliens had their own way of gathering oxygen - or one of the other gases - some through specialised organs, other through their skin. The most striking thing about the female was her hair, a mop of curls in shades of red and orange, like flames sprouting from her scalp. It was such a contrast to her pale skin, so white as if all colour had been sucked from it. Standing between the two blue-skinned Kyvens made her look even more exotic.

Did all humans look that way? If so, I'd quite like to visit their planet. This female was gorgeous.

I zoomed in a little to see her more clearly. She stared at everything as if she'd never been on a shuttle before. Her pink lips were slightly parted. Was that pink natural? I wanted to touch her lips to find out.

"Cargo is loaded," Katak reported through the intercom. I quickly switched to a different screen, feeling a little guilty over checking out the passengers. I'd get to see more of them soon enough, once we reached the PoTA-2.

HEATHER

The ship was bigger than the one that had transported us to Kyven all those months ago. A shuttle had collected Sahra, Abby, and me from the planet's surface and had taken us into orbit where the PoTA-2 was waiting. Abby and her Kyven mate were holding hands as we followed the shuttle's pilot through the hangar. She was a Kyven woman who had said barely anything throughout our walk. Her hair was dyed bright green, unless it was natural? I'd only ever seen Kyvens with blue hair until now. If she'd been a little more friendly, I would have asked if that was her real hair colour, but she didn't seem interested in conversation.

We left the huge hangar and started walking along a dimly lit corridor. Our baggage was still in the shuttle; the pilot had told us it would be transported to our cabins by bots. Something squeaked behind me and I whirled around only to find a pink ball of fluff bumping against my shoe. What on Earth?!

"Jiji!" the pilot exclaimed, showing emotion for the first time. She picked the pink ball up and smothered it against her chest. "I missed you."

The thing squeaked again and became even fluffier, if that was possible. Was that a pet? I couldn't see any trace of eyes, a mouth or even paws among all the pink hair that sprouted in all directions.

Without any kind of explanation, our guide continued walking, clearly expecting us to follow. The pink fluffball squeaked every few seconds, a sound as irritating as sneakers catching on rubber floor. By the time we finally got to a set of large double doors, I was ready to throttle that squeak-thing. If it even had a neck to throttle.

The pilot held her wrist against a sensor on the wall and the doors slid open, revealing a circular room beneath a glass dome. It reminded me of a planetarium, with stars sparkling all around us, except that these stars were real. One of those tiny bright dots was the sun, our sun. For a moment, I felt dizzy as I realised just how vast space really was. I'd felt exactly the same during our journey to Kyven. I'd felt small and unimportant, like an ant crawling on the ground without any knowledge of the world beyond her anthill. How many civilisations were out there? How many people, how many aliens were staring at the stars this very second?

"Welcome to the PoTA-2. I'm Captain Ellabee," a smooth voice said.

I turned my attention to the three aliens in front of us. Two were seated at consoles, but the one that drew my gaze was the captain standing in the centre of the room. Her skin was a darker shade of blue than that of the Ta-Kavalla sisters, a deep midnight blue with a purple hue. Her braided hair was the opposite, the colour of a bright summer's sky, so pale it was almost white. Tiny golden beads graced the ends of her many braids. She had a don't-mess-with-me sort of look, enhanced by the metal bands around her biceps, the dozens of piercings in her pointy ears and the leather coat she wore over her simple black clothes.

"Ellabee, good to see you," Sahra greeted the captain. "Thanks for making this detour."

"We were in the area. Besides, if what your sister says is true, it'll be worth our time. Earth goods are a rarity that will make us good money on the black market."

Yes, definitely a pirate. Or at least a rogue.

"This is my mate Abby and this is Heather, another human," Sahra introduced us.

I tried hard not to cringe. *Another human.* Was that all I was to them?

"Welcome," Captain Ellabee said with a smirk as if she found something amusing. "While you're on the PoTA-2, you live by my rules. They're simple. Do what I say. Do what my crew say. Don't kill anyone. Don't steal. Stay out of the way of the crew. Don't mess with the bots. And finally, enjoy yourselves. You look like you need a bit of fun."

She looked at me while saying that last bit, that amused grin still curving her purple lips.

"I wonder what she meant by that," I muttered to nobody in particular. While I got on perfectly fine with Sahra and Abby, I didn't really know them. They both worked at the animal park the Ta-Kavalla sisters owned and Abby had been a veterinarian back on Earth and she'd checked out our animals when we first arrived but I hadn't really got to socialise much with her beyond that. Like every mated couple, they existed in a bubble that left someone like me on the outside. Just like Rachel and Tamsia, I thought bitterly.

I was happy for my cousin that she'd found someone, there was no doubt about it, but it was weird to be on the outside. Rachel and I had grown up together, I considered her my sister, but now she had a life of her own and I needed to adapt.

"Time to get off the bridge," Captain Ellabee commanded. "Crew only during launches. You can sit in the lounge for now until someone shows you to your cabins."

We hurried back along the corridor we'd come from when something hit my legs and I looked down, finding the little pink squeaky thing rubbing itself against my shoes.

Two blue hands scooped the creature up from the floor and the pilot with the green hair smiled at me. Her eyes weren't blue like the other Kyvens either, instead they were emerald green and sparkled just as much. It made them stand out even more against her deep blue skin. "Sorry about that. He's not usually like this. Jiji must like you."

"Thanks, I think?" I studied the fuzzy ball, trying to figure out where its front and back was. "What is it?"

"A qoark."

"I don't know what that is." I stared at the qoark, whatever that meant. "Is it a pet?"

"What's a pet?" the pilot asked in return.

"An animal friend that lives in your house," I explained. The translator software definitely needed another upgrade.

"Oh, then yes. But he mostly lives in my cabin." She ran her free hand through her striking green hair, making it ripple like seaweed on a coral reef or maybe grass in the wind.

I blushed when she noticed me staring.

"You like my hair?" she asked with a knowing grin.

"I've only seen Kyvens with blue hair so far," I replied, although admittedly, I hadn't seen that many of them. Just the Ta-Kavalla sisters and a handful of others who had visited their animal park, but they were all rather plain looking. Very different from the green-haired pilot or the pirate captain.

The pilot chuckled. "One of my parents was Kyvarak."

"Ah." I didn't know what the significance of that was. "Sorry, I don't know what Kyv..."

"Kyvarak. I believe it can be translated as one-who-walks-underwater."

That raised more questions than it answered but I had a funny feeling she could explain things to me the entire flight, and I'd be none the wiser. This was a completely different world and as exciting as it was to discover it, it was daunting at the same time. It reminded me of how I'd felt when my parents died and I felt lost in the world without anyone to guide me.

The qoark squeaked loudly again and the pilot nodded, like she could understand what it said. "You're right. It's time, isn't it?" She gave me somewhat of a smile. "We're about to take off, you should find your seat or the captain will give you a full ear."

I smiled at the way she said her warning. I didn't know if there was a similar expression in Kyven or if the translator on my end hadn't done its job, but I got the message.

"Is the captain always like that?" I asked quietly, running under the assumption that the pirate woman wouldn't be able to hear me from all the way up on the bridge. Rachel had never said anything about Tamsia having enhanced hearing but I didn't want to take my chances and get booted off this spaceship.

The pilot chuckled, a lovely bubbly sound. "She is. Go sit, human."

"My name is Heather," I told her firmly. It was one thing for Sahra to refer to me as 'just another human', but I wasn't going to let this stranger call me that.

"Heather," she repeated with a slight lisp and a bit of a smirk. "Go sit, Heather."

Before I could tell her off for mocking me, she was already jogging towards the front of the ship. I looked around to see if Sahra and Abby had any thoughts about my weird interaction with her and her qoark but they were lost in their own world as usual.

No wonder I was striking up conversations with strange women. It would be good once we reached Earth, then maybe I wouldn't feel so alone.

[4]

ATINA

As much as I loved Kyven, there was always something satisfying about leaving its orbit.

"We're nearing the edge of Kyven's gravitational field, secondary left booster is almost warmed up and ready to shift into second gear," I said into my headset, warning Katak so he was ready once we shot into open space.

"Heard, right booster will be ready too. On your signal."

Jiji squeaked demandingly as he bounced up and down my dashboard.

"Not now," I told him, pushing him to the side so I could keep a close eye on the counter, tightening my grip on the lever. "Shifting into second gear in three, two, one." The ship wobbled ever so slightly but held stable as we tore free from Kyven's gravity. "We are in open space, I repeat, we are in open space. Setting course to Planet #47283 and switching to automatic pilot."

"Sounds good to me. All in a day's work," Katak replied, probably already leaning back with his feet up on the dash.

"Feet down," Captain Ellabee commanded icily. "This is the bridge, not your cabin."

He rolled his eyes at me, but made sure that Ellabee couldn't see it. As much as she was strict and bossy, she was also the best captain I'd ever worked for, and I knew Katak felt the same way.

While we went through the standard checks and manoeuvres, I couldn't help but wonder what our passengers were doing just now. I'd shown them to the lounge, a dingy room that didn't deserve that name, before hurrying back to the bridge just in time to avoid Ellabee's anger for being late. Maybe I could give them a tour of the ship later on, once my shift ended. I checked the time. Another two hours. Urgh. Not that I didn't love my job, but right now I wanted to be elsewhere.

But why? What was so fascinating about the passengers that I got all distracted? I never usually cared about guests on the PoTA-2. They were a necessary nuisance who often got in the way of the day to day running of the ship. I'd told Ellabee multiple times that I didn't support her strategy of taking on paying passengers. But today, I felt very different. With the same analytical thinking I usually reserved for difficult manoeuvres, I scrutinised my feelings. I wasn't interested in all three of the guests. Only one. The fire-haired female with the shy smile. Why? She was so different from the females I usually spent time with. She wasn't even Kyven. She seemed to be living on our planet, but I'd gathered from our short interaction that she didn't know much about my kind. She'd looked at me blankly when I'd mentioned Kyvaraks, which meant she was clueless about our history. Granted, there were some Kyvens who didn't know much about Kyvaraks either, but they were usually racist, ignorant or both.

"Atina!" Captain Ellabee snapped. "Why are we flying in a circle?"

I realised my finger was pushing down on the wrong button. Rak. Such a rookie's mistake. I had to focus. Get through this shift. And then find the passengers so I could get the fire-haired female out of my mind.

Once I was able to take a break, I made my way down from the bridge, surprised to find the three females still sitting in the lounge. Nobody had bothered to show them to their cabin.

"Finally!" the Kyven female exclaimed. Had she ever introduced herself? No, she'd told us the names of her companions, but not her own. "I was starting to think we'd have to sleep in here."

I looked around for any other member of my crew who could take over. I only wanted to talk to Heather, not all three of them.

"Are you going to show us to our cabins?" the Kyven asked, no, demanded.

"I suppose I can, although technically I'm on a break. Follow me."

I sighed internally as I led them to the guest cabins. I'd been hoping to have a drink, maybe a meal with the human, not play tourist guide. Why hadn't someone else done this already?

The sleeping quarters were in the starboard section of the ship. The smell of dirty socks wafted from Kayluk's cabin and I fastened my step. The guest cabins were at the end of the corridor, the furthest away from the bridge.

"Both cabins are only big enough for two kyvenoids each, so one of you will have to be on your own," I explained. "There is a small wash cabin in between them, but you can also use the communal washing space. Meal times are whenever the cook feels like making something or whenever the captain gets hungry. It'll be announced with a gong. You really can't miss it. Your baggage should have already been brought to the cabins, but if not, let someone know."

Not me, I begged internally. I had other plans. Like snuggling up with Jiji and eating an entire bowl full of quika crisps. Where was my little qoark? It usually followed me around the PoTA-2, but it looked as if it had stayed on the bridge. Traitor.

"Thank you for doing this," Heather said from behind me. "Sorry we're taking up your break time."

I resisted the urge to turn around and smile at her.

"No problem at all. And if you have any questions or problems, just ask."

The words slipped out before I could stop myself. I hoped the other two hadn't heard it. I didn't want to become a guide for all three of them.

We finally reached the guest cabins. This corridor had never felt this long before. Abby and the Kyven female disappeared into one of them right away, leaving me alone with Heather.

"This one's yours. Hold your hand against this sensor and it will key itself to you. That way nobody will be able to enter your cabin unless you let them in."

She held her hand against the wall, but not quite on the sensor. Without thinking, I took her hand and gently moved it to the right place. Her skin was so soft, her fingers so slender. My dark blue skin was a sharp contrast to her almost white complexion.

The sensor beeped, signalling that it had finished the adjustment. The door slid open, revealing a small yet clean cabin with two fold-down beds, a few cubby holes and a large screen on the wall opposite that currently showed the spacescape we were travelling through.

"It's not very big, but at least you don't have to share." Why was I apologising to her?

"It's perfect," Heather said with a smile. "How do I lower the bed?"

I showed her the button. As if by accident, our fingers touched again. My ears grew hot and I quickly withdrew.

"Anyway, do you need anything else?"

A strange rumbling sound interrupted her before she could reply. She glanced down at her stomach while her cheeks filled with colour. "Sorry. I think I'm hungry. Breakfast was quite a while ago."

"Does your body always tell you that you need food?" I asked curiously.

"Just sometimes. I hadn't realised Kyvens don't have stomach rumbles, but I suppose I've not spent all that much time with... Anyway, is there somewhere I can get a snack? I forgot to pack any."

She looked around for her baggage. For a moment, I wished that it hadn't been delivered yet only so I could help her search for it. I chastised myself for those thoughts.

"You can get food in the lounge where you were sitting earlier."

I hurried away before I felt tempted to offer to show her the way.

Why was I becoming so obsessed with this kyvenoid?

[5]

After what felt like a few days on the spaceship, I was slowly finding my way around. There wasn't much to explore between my cabin, the food hall, and the observation deck, but I kept discovering new mysteries.

I pressed my hand firmly on the food hatch's touchpad, frustration coursing through me when it flashed all kinds of dots at me. The implanted translator did an adequate job in helping me around but it was useless when it came to written media.

My stomach grumbled impatiently and I searched around for someone to help me, my gaze latching onto the green-haired pilot coming from the bridge. I didn't know her name and while she'd initially been rather stoic and stiff, she had also been the only one who'd bothered to show us to our bunks.

"Hey." I waved pathetically, hoping to get her attention. I still didn't know her name.

A lopsided smile tugged her blue lips up as she came my way. "Hello, Heather."

My stomach fluttered from the way she said my name but that could've also just been the hunger. "I'm trying to get a snack but it's not working."

"That's because this is a tool cabinet." The pilot gestured to a similar sized hatch a few metres to the left. "That one is for food outside of meal times."

"Oh." Embarrassed, I made my way over to the other hatch and pressed my palm on the pad again, frustrated when nothing happened here either.

"You're still doing it wrong." The pilot placed her hand on mine, just like before again. "You need to move your fingers, like this."

A spark danced up my arm from her touch and I could feel the heat rushing to my cheeks and ears, no doubt turning them a bright shade of red. I always hated how easily my skin flushed but there wasn't much I could do about it.

I did as she asked and the pad lit up while an automated voice inside my head asked what I wanted to eat. Of course, I thought of burgers, pizza, and ice cream.

In return, the spaceship dropped a plate of green goop that had a concerning wobble like jelly or aspic.

I pulled my nose up. "What's that?"

"Ship guts," the green-haired Kyven replied. "It's good for you."

"Is it really edible or is this another tool cabinet?"

To prove her point, the pilot leaned down and took a playful bite from the top of the jelly. "It tastes better than it looks."

Part of me just wanted to throw it in the bin but my rumbling stomach reminded me that I'd regret that later. Reluctantly, I nibbled on the edge, trying to ignore how weirdly slippery and smooth it was. A sour taste spread through my mouth, followed by a horrid bitterness that reminded me of the time I tried to eat a roasted coffee bean.

"I can't believe I'm saying this, but it does not taste better than it looks," I said once I'd managed to swallow. My stomach turned just thinking about taking another bite. I couldn't. "I can't eat this."

"Here, try this." The pilot handed me something similar to a protein bar in a see-through wrapper.

"Are you sure?" While it looked better, I was still cautious as I took my first bite of the crunchy bar. A welcome sweetness exploded on my tongue and instantly erased the lingering bitterness from the jelly. "Mmm, yum. That reminds me of my favourite candy bar. Wow, that's so good. Where did you get that from?"

"Home," the other woman replied with a shrug.

"It's amazing. Thank you." I quickly devoured the whole thing. If I'd known the food was going to be so bad, I'd have brought my own. At least now I knew to bring a whole lot of snacks back with me on the return journey.

Once my immediate hunger was stilled, I could

think straight again. I still didn't know the pilot's name and she'd already helped me twice.

"I don't think I caught your name," I told her.

"Why would you catch my name? It's not on the run," she replied with a confused frown.

"It's an expression in my language. I meant, I don't know your name."

"That's correct," she said with a little grin, clearly enjoying herself.

"What is your name?"

"No, What is not my name." A flash of pink shot past us and bounced up against the wall, landing on the pilot's shoulder. She smiled warmly at the qoark and tickled its belly. Or face. "Hello, Jiji. You finally decided to join me?"

The fluffy animal squeaked like a cat toy that was being massacred.

"Aww, you silly thing."

I yelped when it jumped on my shoulder and rubbed its soft pink far against my face. It reminded me a little of the softest lamb wool, but just in a nauseating colour. It kind of looked like a ball of wool, too.

"Jiji likes you."

"I don't know why," I told her, gently lifting the qoark up and holding it in my hands so I could study it. Up close, I could make out a pair of beady eyes hidden deep within the fur and a tiny mouth that looked a little like an octopus beak. It was a weird creature that seemed to hold a lot of affection for the pilot.

It made me miss my sheep. It was a shame I

couldn't bring them with me but totally understandable; there were too many of them and they weren't exactly well-behaved. Mocha always peed on my shoes and Cloudling liked nibbling on my shirt, but they'd been with me ever since my parents died. I'd never been separated from them for very long.

This trip better be worth it.

"I still don't know your name," I said when I felt the pilot's gaze on me.

"Maybe it should stay that way. It's kind of fun."

"It's not fun for me. I don't like having a conversation with someone if I don't know their name."

Her eyes lit up with mirth. "Oh, you want to have a conversation with me?"

I looked around the empty room. There was nobody else to talk to. Abby and Sahra were in their cabin, and I didn't really want to imagine what they were doing. I doubted Captain Ellabee would like it if I went to the bridge and pestered her with questions. I didn't feel tired yet, so this nameless pilot was as good as anyone to pass the time with.

"Maybe. If you have another of those crunchy bars."

With a grin, the green-haired woman produced one from her pocket. "I always have at least a few of them with me. You never know when you get hungry."

She handed me the bar and picked up Jiji, depositing the fluffy animal on her shoulder. It squeaked adorably before making sounds that reminded me of smacking lips. Was it kissing the pilot? It was hard to see under all that pink fur.

I nibbled on my bar, not really hungry anymore. The first had been more filling than I'd realised.

"Where is everyone?" I asked when the pilot stayed silent.

"Working, sleeping, stargazing. Take your pick. We're always busiest after a planet stop, so most of the crew will be hard at work. You'll find more people in the lounge later, once all the cargo has been unpacked and sorted. Then everything calms down until we get close to the next destination."

"And what is our next destination? Earth?"

"No, Andui'li, a moon of planet X6827. The planet itself is uninhabited, which is why it never got a proper name, but the moon is a popular holiday destination. We've got some cargo to offload there. I hope we get a bit of shore leave. They have these amazing creamy treats there that are served in a seashell. Sooooo good. And the views from the top of the spaceport are amazing. Sometimes I just sit there and take in the view."

"That sounds very relaxing."

She grinned. "It really is. I need to ask the captain if we get to spend some time on the moon. If we do, I suppose I could show you around. If you have the right documents. They don't let everyone land there. Scared of people settling permanently instead of just staying for a holiday."

That sounded surprisingly like some countries back home. I supposed it shouldn't come as a surprise that planets had immigration controls and all that. They'd scanned our biometric information at the spaceport on Kyven, but I hadn't needed any documents. Not that I had any. When we'd left Earth, we hadn't exactly planned to end up on an alien planet. Did they have space passports? Alien visas? I'd have to ask Sahra. She'd travelled a lot and would know.

Jiji snored loudly. I looked at the pilot and we both started laughing.

"I'm Atina, by the way."

I held out my hand. "Nice to meet you, Atina."

ATINA

I stared at her hand. What did she want me to do? Did she want another nutrient bar? Two should have been enough to sustain her for a day. Unless her metabolism worked completely differently from other kyvenoids, she should be full.

"What do you want?" I asked when she didn't offer an explanation.

She slapped her hand against her forehead, confusing me even more. "Sorry! I keep forgetting that Kyvens don't shake hands. You'd think I'd have learned after months of living on your planet, but it just won't stick in my brain. It's the one thing I can't unlearn."

"Why do you shake hands? Is it a ritual?"

For a moment, I hoped that it might be a mating ritual, but then discarded that thought immediately. I didn't have time for a mate. And she likely wasn't interested anyway.

"Shaking hands is a way of greeting someone," Heather explained. "It's the first step of getting to know someone."

I held out my right hand like she had done. With a smile, she took mine and moved it up and down in a flowing motion. Curious.

"And now you know me?" I asked. "What did that movement teach you about me?"

Heather frowned. Nice, that was a gesture our two species had in common, unless it meant something else for humans.

"It didn't teach me anything. Should it have?"

Now we were both confused. Luckily, Jiji interrupted us with another loud snore. I readjusted it a little, making sure it didn't fall off my shoulder now that it was fast asleep. The little qoark trusted me completely, even in its sleep. It had taken a long time for it to become this trusting and loving, but it had been worth all the effort.

"She is so cute," Heather gushed. "How long have you had her?"

"Since before I joined this crew. I found it in a dirty cage on a Kwilen market, caked in mud. Jiji was so thin it barely weighed anything. I persuaded the owner to sell it to me. We've been best friends ever since."

I didn't mention all the sleepless nights during which I'd worried about whether Jiji would survive, nor the crazy vet-med bills, nor the reaction of my previous captain who'd told me to get rid of it. Obviously, I hadn't. Instead, I'd found a new ship and a new captain, and life was better for it.

"Do you have a lot of traditions on your planet?" I asked, not sure what about the pink kyvenoid intrigued me so much. Maybe it was the way she floated around the spaceship, kind of going around without much purpose.

I wondered what that was about.

Heather chuckled, a delightful sound. "You have no idea. Traditions is the name of the game on Earth."

"Your traditions are games?"

"No, it's another expression."

She seemed to have a lot of those as well, which made no sense. What was the point of communication if they dedicated secret meaning to their sentences? It made me wonder if I interpreted anything she said so far correctly.

My controlband on my wrist chimed, an alert from my cockpit that something needed my attention which was a shame. I was enjoying my conversation with Heather, even if she was hard to understand. That was partially what made her intriguing to me. She was like a living puzzle and I liked those.

"I have to go," I said, gesturing in the direction of the bridge.

Heather seemed dejected, although it was hard to read her facial expressions. "That's a pity. Thank you for the cereal bar."

Cereal. Another word I didn't understand but I

appreciated her gratitude. I didn't know if that was a thing on her planet or if she'd picked it up on Kyven but it was nice to know that she was capable of having complex emotions, unlike some of the other aliens I sometimes came into contact with.

"What are you going to do next?" I asked, ignoring the alarm for a moment. It couldn't be that important if the sirens weren't going off.

Heather shrugged. "I don't know. Nothing, really. This spaceship is kind of boring, no offence."

"It's not my ship," I returned. My alarm chimed again and even though I knew better, I figured, what was the harm? "Want to see my cockpit?"

A snorting sound emitted from Heather that she smothered by covering her mouth with her hands.

"What's so funny?" I asked.

"I don't think I can explain."

"Another expression?"

"Something like that. But yes, I'd like to see your... *cockpit*."

The way she said the word made it clear there was another meaning to it but she wasn't going to share it with me. It just made me more curious to learn more of her Earth language. I'd heard her speak it with the other kyvenoid female, a melodic string of sounds.

Hopefully, I'd have some free time when we docked on her planet so I could explore a bit. I hadn't been before and with good reason, my previous captain wasn't certified to visit planets and moons outside of the Galactic Union.

"Follow me," I told Heather, making my way up the bridge, relieved when Captain Ellabee was nowhere to be found. I didn't think she'd appreciate having a passenger in the command centre but I'd keep a close eye on Heather, make sure she didn't do anything wrong.

Jiji jumped off my shoulder when we got to the cockpit and rolled over to the flashing orange lights, drawn to them like it usually was.

Heather paused behind me. "Is that bad?"

"No, just have to check something." I sat down on my chair and requested a status report, acutely aware of the female standing behind me.

A long log rolled onto my screen with the issue highlighted.

I instantly pressed an alert button to send an alarm to the rest of the crew and reached for my headset. "Katak, are you there?"

No reply. He was probably on his break too.

Behind me, Heather came a step closer. "Is everything okay?"

"Yes, I just need to adjust the course. One of Zatish's moons has drifted from its usual orbit and is in our path." I tried my headset again. "Katak? Are you there?"

I waited a moment before I switched the automatic pilot off and took manual control of the ship. It was risky not to have my co-pilot in his seat for a manoeuvre like this but if I waited much longer, it could put us all in danger. If the system had detected the moon earlier, perhaps there would've been time to recalculate the route but that was even riskier now.

"Are we going to crash?" Heather asked in a shaky voice.

This was why Captain Ellabee told us not to have passengers in the cockpit.

"No. I've never crashed a ship in my life and this won't be the first time. Go back to the bridge and take a seat there. Strap in just in case."

As much as I wanted to keep her close to make sure she was alright, there was only one chair in each cockpit. The two glass spheres bulged from the bridge's side like an insect's eyes, each housing one pilot.

"Katak, I could really do with your help just now," I tried again while Heather hurried to the bridge. I resisted the urge to twist around to check whether she was safely sitting down.

With the autopilot off, the ship's fate lay in my hands. Generally, this wouldn't be much of an issue, but the system had waited too long to send an alert. What was wrong with our sensors? First the shuttle's bumpy landing, now this. Ellabee really had to invest more into repairs. I wasn't willing to risk my life for her profit margin.

I adjusted our course as much as I could, then hailed my co-pilot again. "Katak, if you don't show up right away, I'm going to personally disembowel you."

"Atina?" Finally! He sounded like he'd just woken up. "What's wrong?"

"Everything is rakking wrong. Get here right now!"

"On my way."

At least he'd grasped the urgency of the situation. It didn't take long for me to hear his hurried footsteps. A click later, he appeared on my screens.

"What's the ma... oh no. Where did that moon suddenly come from?"

"I've been asking myself the same question." I gave him a moment to look at the data. "Manoeuvre alpha-22?"

"Yes, that's what I was thinking. We should alert the captain."

I groaned. I'd hoped to keep Ellabee out of this. I didn't want her to cut my wages for something that wasn't my fault. But he was right. This was a dangerous situation. Not quite an about-to-crash-situation, but still very serious.

"You do it," I told him. "She likes you better."

He laughed before doing a group broadcast to the captain's quarters. I grit my teeth and prepared for the manoeuvre, hoping that we'd get out of this with all our bowels intact.

[7]

HEATHER

The cockpits were completely soundproof, so I didn't hear what was going on until Captain Ellabee burst onto the bridge. I found it a little strange that nobody else had been here to keep watch, but then, what did I know about spaceships? Kyven technology was probably so advanced that they didn't need anyone to monitor the bridge.

The captain shot me a surprised look, but then ignored me as she stared at various screens and scrolled through star maps.

"Impossible," she muttered to herself.

I was tempted to get up and sneak away. I shouldn't be here. I was just a passenger and had no skills that would help in this situation. Unless we encountered a herd of alien sheep that needed shepherding, I was useless. Just when I was about to undo the safety belt around my chest and waist, Captain Ellabee pressed a button, and bright green lights began to flash all around us.

"Green alert. Everyone strap in," an automatic voice announced through speakers.

A cold shiver ran down my back. This didn't bode well. I didn't know where green was on the scale of alerts, but Ellabee's expression was serious enough to scare me. I wished Atina was here with me to explain what was going on. I didn't like being out of the loop.

Were Sahra and Abby still in their cabin? There had to be ways to strap in there, maybe on the bed? I hadn't spent any time in my cabin, too impatient to see more of the ship.

A tiny squeak near my right foot made me look down. It was Jiji, its fur even fuzzier than before. Maybe it was scared. I bent down to pet it, but the safety straps prevented me from reaching Jiji.

"Atina is in the cockpit," I whispered to the pink ball of fluff. "But you can stay with me if you want."

It rubbed against my leg, squeaking with excitement. Or was it fear? It was hard to tell while its eyes were hidden under fur. Without warning, Jiji jumped onto my lap - was it jumping if no limbs were involved? - and squeaked again, this time sounding a little happier. I ran my hands over its fur, amazed at just how soft it was. Sheep looked fluffy, but their wool was coarser and always left an oily residue on my fingers. I loved the scent of wool though, one of my favourite aspects of spending all day with sheep. I gave Jiji a tentative sniff. I almost expected it to smell like candy floss, but it didn't have any scent at all. It? She? He? I'd have to ask Atina. Yet another question to add to my list.

"Explain!" Captain Ellabee suddenly snapped. I looked up in shock before realising that she was talking to Atina and another Kyven, both of whom were now showing on a screen.

"The sensors must have been malfunctioning," Atina reported in a calm, professional voice. "I only got an alert when we were already too close to the moon. I'm going to run a full diagnostic once we're out of harm's way."

"And how are we going to get out of harm's way? Half the predictions say we're going to crash."

Goosebumps puckered all over my arms. It was worse than I'd thought.

"We're about to execute manoeuvre alpha-22," the male Kyven explained. "That should let us use the moon's gravitational pull to our advantage and slingshot around it. We'll be off course for a bit, but it will only be a minor delay."

"What are the chances of success?" the captain asked sharply.

Atina didn't cringe under Ellabee's scrutiny. I was proud of her even though I barely knew the pilot. "Eighty per cent."

"Not good enough. Where's Lini?"

This was quickly turning into a full-on disaster and part of me wished I was back in the lounge or wherever Sahra and Abby were, delightfully oblivious to the impending doom. I glanced in the direction of Atina's cockpit, still holding on tightly to little Jiji. The pink fluff ball seemed to have gone to sleep and was now softly purring. At least I could take care of her.

A green alien with a wild mohawk on their otherwise bald head rushed past me, a concerned look on their face. "Here, I've run an initial status report. There's an issue with our network's connectivity, the power has been cutting out temporarily and it's messing with the system."

A look of rage darkened the captain's face. "Rak! You're kidding me? I just had Queri check all of this, he assured me it was all fine and charged me an outrageous fortune for it as well, that bastard. When I see him next, I'm going to rip his bowels out with my bare hands. Wake Inil and get me a solution."

I almost screamed when two eyes opened on the back of Lini's head. A mouth appeared, one without teeth, which was quite possibly the weirdest thing I'd seen and I'd seen a lot of weird things since I got onto that first spaceship. The two-faced alien put its hands on top of the control panel and the eyes on the back of his head glowed red.

"Electrical disturbance detected. Affected ports are A4, 234, and T9. Affected bays are C1, C22, and L4," the mouth said in a monotone voice. "Attempting to reroute energy to affected areas... Reroute failed."

I probably shouldn't be here but the safety belts strapping me in were preventing me from leaving. At least I could see Atina, or rather, the back of her head.

Captain Ellabee paced back and forth with nervous energy. "Okay, start manoeuvre alpha-22."

"Aye, aye, Captain," Atina and her co-pilot said from their respective cockpits, both of them fully focused. Even though I hadn't known her for very long, I felt a little bit better knowing she was steering this ship. She felt like someone reliable who wasn't just going to let us crash.

"Turning off stabilisers in three, two, one—"

The pressure in the ship shifted and I was almost thrown from my seat, only prevented by the safety straps. My eardrums pulsed painfully as we seemed to rise rapidly. A sharp turn made Jiji fly from my arms and it released a long panicked noise that struck my heart. I reached out to her and she came tumbling back towards me as the ship tilted in the opposite direction. This time, I grabbed hold of it and held it tightly in my lap as I curled around it. I wasn't sure exactly who was getting more comfort from this but at least I wasn't alone.

Suddenly, the pressure disappeared and the ship levelled out much to my relief. I opened my eyes, not yet daring to breathe.

"Manoeuvre alpha-22 was successful," the

monotone voice of the green alien declared. "Disengage safety system."

The belts strapping me into the chair without an inch of wiggling room unclicked and I jumped up, glad to be free again.

Captain Ellabee wiped a bead of sweat from her blue forehead. "Great, well done, everyone. Set the course for the nearest maintenance station and someone go check on our cargo, especially the livestock in the bays."

While she barked commands, I quickly hurried towards Atina's cockpit with Jiji still in my arms. The pink fluffball instantly jumped onto the pilot's shoulder and rubbed its body against her.

"Hey, little one." Atina turned around, looking slightly paler than before. "So that's where Jiji went."

"I held onto her for the whole thing. Her? Him?"

"It," she replied, tickling the pet affectionately. "The animals from Kwilen don't have genders. Are you okay? I'm sorry, I should never have brought you here."

"It's okay, it wasn't your fault."

"I'm not so sure about that. Katak and I did the preflight checks and walked around before we departed. Everything looked fine, so I don't understand why there was a system failure. This could've ended really badly, we could've crashed."

I placed a hand on her shoulder, hoping she understood it as reassuring. "But we didn't. So where is the nearest maintenance station?"

"Sivilia, it's a remote planet, mostly used for

agriculture. If we need to replace parts of our ship, it's going be a pain."

"So how long will we be there? When will we get to Earth?"

Atina gave me a wry smile. "I don't know."

$$[\ 8 \ ]$$

ATINA

Sivilia wasn't the worst planet to get stranded on. It was beautiful and calm, but remote and the population didn't take well to foreigners, which was a bit of an issue for the intergalactic crew of the PoTA-2.

I jogged down the loading dock to where Captain Ellabee was chatting with one of the engineers. The captain was a stern woman at the best of times but she looked downright murderous at the moment. I really hoped it wasn't my fault or negligence that caused our system to malfunction like this.

The captain looked up when she saw me. "Atina. You flew well."

"Thank you." I gestured back at the ship. "What happened?"

"I'm running a full diagnostic scan now but it's

looking like some sort of virus. Best guess? Queri sold me some dodgy parts last time I was there." The way she said his name spelled trouble for him next time she saw him.

"So what now?"

"I'll have to make repairs, so no flying for a while. I need you to gather some people; the malfunctions messed with the livestock bays and the rashipis got out of their enclosure. They're all over the cargo hold. Get them back in their bay."

I wanted to point out that I was a pilot, not a rashipi-sitter, but in a situation like this, it was all hands on deck. I'd just have to find some help to herd what I considered some of the most annoying animals that existed on Kendar. I wasn't sure what planet they were bound to, but they'd made nothing but a huge mess ever since we'd taken the herd on board. I was glad I wasn't usually in charge of our living cargo.

"Maybe ask our passengers," the captain suggested, "I've heard they've got some sort of animal park. Perhaps they'll volunteer to help."

For some reason, having an excuse to spend more time with Heather cheered me up. I checked my controlband for her location. She was in her cabin, which luckily wasn't far from the cargo hold.

When I stood in front of her door, I hesitated. Was I presuming too much? Did she even want to help? Maybe Heather had enough of me after all the excitement she'd had on the bridge. But then I thought of the loose rashipis and how much work it would be to herd them back into their pen. I could do with some company.

As soon as I held my hand against the scanner, I heard a chime announce me inside the cabin. I hoped she knew how to let me in - and yes, the door slid open, revealing the pretty human.

"Hey," she smiled.

"Hey."

We grinned at each other until I remembered just why I'd come here.

"Do you want to me help catch some rashipis? They're loose all over the cargo bay and the captain asked me to herd them back into their enclosure."

"Rashipis?" she asked. "I assume they're animals?"

"Yes, sorry, they're a fairly dumb animal from planet Kendar. They are bred for their fur, it's fluffy and pink and looks like clouds on their planet. They have six stout legs with sharp talons, but they're usually very docile. They're too stupid to fight, basically. When they get loose, they forget where they came from, so it's a pain to find them and bring them back together."

"They don't sound too dissimilar from sheep, except for the talons and the six legs," Heather said cheerfully. "I'll try to help the best I can. If they're anything like sheep, I have a few tricks up my sleeve."

I looked at her shirt until she laughed. "Another expression. I don't literally have anything up my sleeve except my arms."

"They're pretty arms," I blurted. My ears grew hot at the blunder. I was as dumb as a rashipi sometimes.

"Are you ready?" I asked quickly.

"Yes, it's not like I have anything better to do. I was planning to read something before you appeared, but I couldn't even decide on which book to start. This sounds like a much better use for my time."

She followed me down the deserted corridors. The rest of the crew were either hard at work or using the unplanned stop for a bit of shore leave. I kind of wished I'd be able to show Heather some of Sivilia instead of chasing after rashipis, but at least I got to spend more time with her. I'd never been this interested in a passenger before. What made her so special? Sure, she was beautiful in an exotic way, but I barely knew her.

As soon as we entered the main cargo hold, the honking of confused rashipis reached my ears. They were making more noise than should be possible.

"Is that them?" Heather shouted to make herself heard over the racket.

"Yes! I'll show you their bay first so you know where to herd them to!"

Everyone else had fled the area and I understood why. It wasn't just the noise. I wanted to cut off my nose to stop the rank smell of rashipi poo. They must have been loose for so long that they'd begun to shit everywhere. Rak. I hoped the captain wouldn't make me clean it up. The bots should be able to deal with that, and if not, I'd get someone to reprogramme them until they could.

"It smells nice in here," Heather exclaimed behind me. "Like Christmas."

I turned around to her to see if she was sarcastic or really meant it. She breathed in deep, her eyes half-closed. Rak, she really seemed to like it.

"Is Christmas an animal on your planet?" I asked, trying to hide my disgust.

"An animal?" She laughed before taking another deep, indulging breath. "No, it's a religious celebration in the winter. There are certain smells I associate with it... cinnamon, berries, ginger, chestnuts... This scent is like all of them combined. It's heavenly."

I decided on the spot that I never wanted to visit Earth during Christmas. Why would anyone want to celebrate to the stink of rashipi poo?

A bang to my left made me whirl around. Something was moving behind a large crate, hopefully a rashipi.

"Rak, I was planning to pick up some of their favourite treats from their enclosure first, but I suppose we'll have to try and capture this one without. Just make sure to stay clear of its talons. And they like it if you scratch their ears. It makes them even more docile."

I slowly walked around the crate until the animal came into view. It was a youngling still, its fur still pale in places. They only turned a bright pink when they reached maturity. This should be fairly easy. Young rashipis instinctively followed anyone who was bigger than them. Stupid as rak.

I waved my arms to get its attention. It cocked its head, dumbly staring at me.

"Good little rashipi," I cooed. "Come with me. Yes, that's it, follow me."

It walked slowly, almost stumbling over its own feet from time to time. Rashipis had been bred for the quality of their fur, not their intelligence. I knew a few people like that too.

The little ball of fur paused, distracted by some of the crying of the other rashipis and darted off in the wrong direction.

"Nooo, come back!" I chased after it, which only seemed to frighten it and scattered all of them even more. This was going to take us forever.

[9]

HEATHER

I watched Atina chase after the rashipis with mild amusement. I'd seen plenty of people attempt to herd sheep before like that, mostly over-enthusiastic children, but I appreciated her commitment as she grabbed one of the pink fluff balls by their torso and physically wrangled her towards the bay. That wasn't uncommon either with unruly sheep who didn't want to be sheared.

And from what I could see so far, these rashipis seemed similar enough. Docile and friendly, easily spooked, but with bright colours that any fantastic knitter would kill to get their hands on.

I clapped my hands as a test, pleased when some of the rashipis looked in my direction while others startled and moved away from the noise. If they were receptive to sounds, that would make my job much easier. I just needed some help.

Over by the bay, Atina had managed to push her one rashipi into the bay and had closed the hatch behind it, making what I was planning impossible. She wasn't paying much attention to me though, and was instead dragging another six-legged animal along, which seemed particularly feisty.

"Atina?" I called, making her look up from her personal wrestling battle.

"Yes?" she panted back, the beads of sweat on her forehead glistening like diamonds. She was truly beautiful.

"Can you stop that for a moment?" I asked. As much as I appreciated her attempt, she was only scattering the animals more and creating mild panic in their vacant eyes.

The green-haired pilot looked confused but let her feisty rashipi go, which darted off as fast as its six legs allowed. Atina came over to me, already looking exhausted and like she needed a strong cup of tea, not that that was a thing on Kyven.

Maybe once we reached Earth, I could introduce her to one of life's simple but best pleasures.

"Do you have any food for the rashipis?"

"There should be some in one of the coolers."

"Should we feed them?"

"I don't know, I'm not an expert on these rakking animals."

I chuckled at her frustration. "Okay, no need to

curse. Can I check out the food? If we can put some in their bay, they might be more inclined to move there."

Afctina's face cleared up instantly. "Right, that makes sense. Good idea." She brought the controlband on her wrist to her mouth. "Lini, can you open the cooler for me? Specifically the one that has the food for the rashipis in it."

A light to my left flashed on and a hatch opened with a hiss, releasing the smell of cinnamon and clove. So that was why the rashipis smelled like Christmas. It had to be because of their food.

Atina went in first and waved me along into the cooler that definitely wasn't cold anymore.

"This smells amazing," I said, wishing I could stay here forever.

Atina pinching her nose shut suggested that she disagreed with me. "It's horrid."

"Not to me." I picked a handful of the long hay and carried it back to the cargo hold where the rashipis were still scattered. A few of them looked up with interest when they noticed me carrying in their food but none were so foolish as to follow me. Maybe if I kept working with them, I could cultivate a good relationship with them, but right now, I was a stranger carrying food but also danger.

I dropped the handful of hay in the back of their enclosure and scattered some around the entrance. One brave rashipi had a little nibble which confirmed I could definitely use it as a lure.

"Let's transport a good portion of this to the bay," I

suggested to Atina. "Is there some kind of cart around that we can use?"

"I don't know, I'm a pilot."

"Well, I'm a shepherd so this is my job." I looked around and found something on wheels that would work. I didn't know if that was meant for it, but it would have to do.

Atina and I loaded it with the Christmas hay, even if she seemed appalled by the smell, she bravely put up with it. I wondered what she'd think of other Earth smells and how she perceived my scent.

We wheeled a good amount of food into the bay, our actions attracting the attention of some of the rashipis who were watching us with a dazed stare. If they were anything like sheep, they were probably a lot cleverer than they looked.

"So what now?" Atina asked when we'd created a nice pile of hay.

"Now we herd. We should close off hatches and corridors so we restrict their path and build some sort of funnel to guide them into the bay." I scanned the cargo hold but there wasn't really anything that could be used as a makeshift barrier. "Actually, scrap that. You'll have to be my funnel."

Confusion painted Atina's adorable face. "I don't understand what we're doing."

"You'll just have to trust me," I told her, feeling confident for the first time I'd got onto this spaceship. I might not know anything about flying, space food, but I knew how to herd. And these rashipis were going to do exactly what I wanted them to do. I was going to make sure of that.

I took Atina by the hand, trying to ignore how nice it felt in mine. She let me pull her towards the entrance of the bay and I positioned her so she blocked the rashipis escape.

"You stand here. Hold out your arms like that." I pushed her arms up, letting my hands slide up her body. "When the first rashipis come your way, just remain calm and kind of... steer them into the bay."

Atina was watching me with interest but I wasn't sure if she'd properly registered what I was saying. Her gaze seemed locked onto my lips and I wondered if she was just trying to understand me better or if she had another motive.

I kind of hoped the latter. I wouldn't be opposed to having some Kyven fun of my own. Seeing my cousin with her Kyven girlfriend - no, mate, I should use the proper term - quite often made me wish for a partner of my own. I'd assumed that one day, I might meet the woman of my dreams on Kyven, but if this space journey ended up as a matchmaking trip, I wouldn't complain. Atina was fun to be around, intelligent, beautiful and exotic. And she clearly liked spending time with me, otherwise she wouldn't have asked me to join her first on the bridge and now on this wild goose...I mean, rashipi hunt.

"...talons?"

I blinked, realising I hadn't heard a word of what Atina had said.

"Sorry, what?"

"I said, what if they swipe at me with their talons?"

"They won't. Herding is not about making animals behave through fear, but through respect. They will know that we're in charge and will follow our commands if we show them that we're the top rashipis."

Atina snorted. "I don't want to be a rashipi. They stink."

"Just an honorary rashipi until they're back in their pen, after that you can be a lovely Kyven again."

"Lovely? You think I'm lovely?"

My cheeks grew hot and I quickly turned to look at one of the lost rashipis instead. "We should get started before they wander even further. Stand here and make yourself look as big as possible. Don't let any rashipis pass. I'll let you know what to do next when I get there."

I walked away as fast as possible to avoid her seeing my embarrassment. One of the rashipis had made it all the way to the other end of the cargo bay, staring at a container with a dazed expression. I wished I had some sheep dogs at my disposal. They would have made my life a whole lot easier, but I'd learned to shepherd both with dogs and without.

I could hear my father's voice echoing in my head. "Always move a sheep slowly, calmly and quietly. Stay outside its flight zone or it might panic. Keeping calm is half the herding done."

Realising I was smiling at the memory, I slowly approached the rashipi.

"Hey, little one. Are you lost? I will help you back.

Smell this food? Yes, there's more of that where it came from. Just follow me and I will take you to the food."

The rashipi sniffed loudly, then trumpeted with what I hoped was hunger. It moved towards me, its legs almost tripping each other as it walked. Another animal nearby had heard the sound and stared at me with curiosity.

"Yes, join us, you can have all the hay you want. Yummy Christmas hay. Just follow me."

Herding could be done by making them follow or by leading them from behind. This was the easier method, so I hoped it would work. My own herd of sheep was trained to follow my voice commands as well as react to the sound of their feed bucket, but I didn't know how the rashipis would behave. Hopefully, they were similar enough to sheep.

By the time I got back to Atina, I had six rashipis following me in their strange uneven gait.

"Just stay there so they don't walk in the wrong direction," I told her without taking my eyes off my herd. "No fast movements. Once we've passed, slowly follow us so you can close the doors of the pen."

"Aye, aye, Captain of the Rashipis," she quipped, clearly enjoying this more now than she'd let on earlier. "I have to say, they suit you."

I wasn't sure if it was a compliment, but I'd take it. I loved being surrounded by animals, alien or from Earth. Once the rashipis were safely locked in their pen, I would see if one of them would let me touch it. I needed to know if its wool was as soft as it looked.

Checking every few metres that the rashipis were still following me, I led them to their pen. I put down my hay in one corner and watched with glee as the first animal started munching on it. The others caught on quickly and hurried to get into the pen so that they wouldn't miss out on food.

With a click, the door closed behind Atina. "There are a few more rashipis to catch, but I think we've earned ourselves a break. Want a snack? No, ignore that, it stinks too much in here to eat."

I couldn't understand how she didn't like the spicy scent of cinnamon and cloves wafting through the air. I could have bathed in it. Even so, everyone had their preferences. "We should finish dealing with all the rashipis first but then we could eat a snack somewhere else. Do you have more of those cereal bars?"

"How about we go for a meal instead?" Atina asked.

I couldn't tell if that was her way of asking me on a date, but it didn't matter, my answer was all the same. "Yes, that sounds lovely."

ATINA

I'd have preferred to take Heather somewhere nice but in a port like this, there wasn't much choice. We ended in a small place with cheap but cheerful food. While Sivilia wasn't known for its cuisine, there were some local dishes that were worth trying.

Heather hummed as she checked out the menu list. "I don't know what any of this is."

"Most of it is good. I wouldn't recommend the follak though."

"Why not?"

"Oh, it's a mixture of ground organ meat and some type of grain cooked in intestines. It's kind of gross and the texture is weird."

Heather's face lit up. "Sounds like haggis."

"And that's a good thing?"

"I love it. I want to try the... What did you call it?"

"Follak." Just saying the name made me shudder. "You're not seriously going to try it?"

"You bet I am. I like the food on Kyven but there are some specialties from home I miss. Haggis is definitely one of them." She seemed genuinely excited by the prospect of trying it.

With a shrug, I ordered the follak for Heather and something more palatable for myself, a double portion in case she didn't like hers so I could share it with her. If not, I'd take the leftovers to my cabin and have them as a snack later on.

The food arrived quickly and I couldn't say her sausage smelled particularly nice, but just like with the rashipis, Heather seemed delighted. She inhaled deeply and released an appreciative hum. "This smells so good. So savoury and herby."

I watched as she took her first bite from the patty, curious if she would actually enjoy it.

"Oh, that's so good! Not quite like haggis but it's similar enough." She closed her eyes and moaned in delight, conjuring inappropriate images in my mind.

To distract myself, I focused my attention on my own food, a typical Sivilian stew that was good for health. "Thank you for helping me with the rashipis, by the way. I'm not sure how I would've managed by myself."

Heather's face was pure bliss. "Of course, I know my way around herd animals. And they behaved like sheep so it was easy enough."

"What are sheep?" I asked.

"They look a little like rashipi, but with white or black fur. They only have four legs with hooves and they're adorable. They're the best cuddlers. If you ever have the opportunity, you should try it."

"If they're anything like rashipis, maybe not. I'd rather cuddle you." The words left my mouth before I fully thought them through.

Heather gave me a shy smile. "I could be on board with that. So how long do you think we'll be stuck here?"

"It depends on how long it takes to fix the ship. I believe the captain and some of the maintenance crew are sorting out the electrical issue and we'll have to restock our supplies as well."

I sat up straighter when I noticed Captain Ellabee enter the eatery. I hadn't expected her at a place like this but then again, she didn't have much more choice than we did.

To my surprise, the captain came our way and paused by our table. "I saw you got the rashipis from the cargo hold already. Impressive, I thought it would take much longer."

"Heather knew how to handle them," I replied, nodding at my companion to give her the credit she deserved.

"I work with animals everyday," Heather explained.

Captain Ellabee's gaze shifted. "Hmm, interesting. I didn't realise we had an animal wrestler onboard."

"I prefer the term shepherd or farmer."

"Alright then, shepherd. When we drop off the rashipis on Figi, you'll help," the captain said in a matter-of-factly tone. With a curt nod, she made her way to the counter to pick up her order and left.

I breathed a sigh of relief once she was gone and rubbed my stomach, as a way to reassure myself I still had all my bowels. While Ellabee wasn't as cruel as my last captain, she could be stern and I knew how quickly patience and tempers were lost.

Heather seemed unbothered by the interaction. Maybe her translator hadn't fully captured the intensity of the conversation.

"She's so impressive," Heather remarked with a dreamy note in her voice.

Jealousy curled through me. "You think?"

"Yes, I saw her in action during the emergency. She really took control. It was both scary but amazing to watch." Heather took another bite from her follak. "You were super impressive too."

"Oh?"

"Yeah, I would not be able to keep calm during a situation like that. The only reason I was somewhat coherent was because I had Jiji to take care of."

"Jiji helps me too," I admitted. "Whenever I feel lonely or miss home, I have my qoark to take my mind off things. Jiji is a special little companion. Sometimes I could swear it knows what I think. That's stupid, I know."

"Not stupid at all. I feel the same way about my sheep. They seem to sense whenever I'm sad and are extra cuddly during those times. Our cat is the same way. When I'm homesick, Timothy will come and curl up on my lap or lick my face. Animals feel more than we give them credit for."

"What's a cat?" I asked curiously.

For some reason, Heather laughed. "How to describe a cat? If you asked him, he'd tell you he's a ferocious predator who has trained us humans to be his faithful servants. If you ask me, he's an adorable fluff ball who is so cute that I can't help but spoil him."

"If he's a ferocious predator, he must be big."

"Not at all. His ego is much bigger than his body. He's about this big-" she held out her hands in front of her, indicating an animal not even as wide as my hips - "and has four legs, a tail, two triangular ears and... wait, I can show him to you. I've got pictures of him on my controlband."

She scrolled through her smart device's gallery until a holographic image of an orange animal appeared between us.

"It doesn't look like a predator," I admitted.

"That's because you haven't felt his claws yet." Heather laughed. "There are bigger versions of house cats that are actual wild predators. We have tigers at the animal park that could kill you if they chose to. Maybe you should come by one day and I can show you around."

"Are you going to feed me to the taygers?" I joked.

Heather grinned widely. "Only if you make me really, really angry."

"It's a date."

Her eyebrows moved up, making her eyes look bigger. Huh, what a fun trick. Human facial muscles were clearly more advanced than Kyven. "Did you just ask me on a date?"

"Technically it was you who invited me."

"You're right. So let's say we both asked. And yes, it's a date."

We grinned at each other. A warm, fuzzy feeling spread through my belly. I liked it. I wanted to feel more of that.

I didn't quite know what to say next. Yes, we'd arranged to go on a date, but that wasn't going to be until we returned to Kyven. What were we going to do until then? Pretend that I wasn't crazily excited? Assume we were just friends?

This was awkward.

"This is slightly awkward," Heather said.

I couldn't help but laugh.

"What?"

"I just thought exactly the same."

"Oh. Great minds."

Was she giving me a compliment? "You have a great mind too," I said, just in case.

"Sorry, another human expression. The full saying is 'great minds think alike'. It's what you say when two people come up with the same thing at the same time. Like we just did."

So not a compliment after all. Or maybe it was? This was confusing.

My controlband vibrated, showing an incoming message from the captain.

"Rak," I cursed. "Captain Ellabee has found several more escaped rashipis. We have to go back and deal with them."

Heather didn't look as frustrated about that as I felt. She popped the last bite of follak into her mouth and got up, clearly desperate to return to the stinky animals. Oh well. I would use the time to think of a way to bring our first date forward. I didn't want to wait any longer than absolutely necessary.

[11]

HEATHER

By the time every single rashipi was back in its pen, I was covered in hay and drenched in sweat. Atina didn't look much better, although I felt like she'd enjoyed herding the animals almost as much as I had. I'd taught her some more tricks on how best to control them, so that she'd have an easier time dealing with them the next time they escaped. I felt a pang of sadness at the thought of her wrangling the rashipis by herself. I'd be back on Kyven with my cousin and her mate's family, while Atina was travelling through space.

Was there even a future for us? Should I be this excited for our date, or should I end things now before they got any further?

"I need a shower," I announced while pulling some hay from my hair.

"Yes, let's get cleaned up. I'll check with the captain to see if we're going to be staying on Sivilia for a little longer. If the repairs take a while, I could take you to this viewing platform on the very top of the Gliua Mountains. The views are breathtaking," Atina said, sounding quite hopeful.

"That sounds lovely," I answered. I had no idea what to expect but just getting to spend a bit more time with the beautiful pilot seemed fun. Even if it only lasted for this round trip to Earth, I was having more fun than I had in a long time.

On my way to my cabin, I ran into Abby coming from hers. The veterinarian smiled in relief. "Oh, there you are. Are you okay? You look..." She gestured at my hair. "Like you've been through the wringer."

"Oh, yes, I'm great," I replied, smiling just thinking back to my rashipi adventure. "Just enjoying my time on the spaceship."

A smirk curled Abby's lip up as she plucked some hay from my hair. "Ooh, I see. Are you discovering how much fun the Kyvens are?"

"No, not like that!" I quickly corrected her before she got the wrong idea. Although I'd be lying if I said I wasn't at least curious to find out in which ways the Kyvens differed from humans, and in which ways they were the same.

Abby seemed mostly bemused. "Well, if you have any questions, you can always ask me. I'm sure you must be curious but it's probably weird to talk about it with your cousin."

I chuckled. "Yes, you can say that. I do *not* want to know anything about Rachel's sex life. Oh, the horror."

"I can only imagine. This is your first time travelling through space since you left Earth, isn't it?"

"It is, it's equal parts exciting and scary. What about you?"

"I've been back and forth a few times. Mostly to see my parents. They don't fully understand why I've moved so far away and they think I live somewhere in Greenland with Sahra. Luckily, they hate the cold so they're quite happy never visiting."

"Really?" Surprise bubbled up in me. "I didn't realise you still got to see your parents."

"Yes, unlike Tilly or you guys, I'm not missing or wanted. I still own my share of the veterinarian practice and I'm registered there as my home address as well. If someone came to check out my exact living details, they'd discover it doesn't make sense but who is going to do that? Nobody cares about what I do." Abby seemed quite happy about that. "Anyway, I'll let you shower. You look like you need it. Sahra and I are having dinner later in the canteen, you're welcome to join us."

"Thanks." Part of me was surprised that Abby had invited me. Despite living close to the Ta-Kavalla sisters, I didn't spend much time with them or the humans living there. I usually kept to myself and so did they, but getting to talk without the translator humming in my ear was refreshing and made me realise I wouldn't be opposed to actually striking up a neighbourly friendship with them.

This trip was shaping up good for all sorts of things.

I pressed my hand on the scanner of my cabin which opened the door and locked it behind me. It wasn't much in terms of private space but the sleeping pod was relatively nice and there was a tiny little window that was wonderful to stare out of when I tried to fall asleep.

The attached bathroom was small as well, but efficient. I stripped my clothes and tossed them into the sanitiser, a handy gadget that I wished we had on Earth. It was so much quicker and more efficient at cleaning my clothes. The shower, however, could benefit from some improvements.

Bracing for the steam, I twisted the knobs and hot water spurted from all sides, cleaning every possible nook, fold, and cranny of my body. It followed it up with a suffocating powder and a spritz of perfume, just for good measure. I'd never felt more cleaner, although slightly violated.

And the towels weren't any better. They were thin and incredibly absorbent, but not fluffy in the slightest and instantly clammy. It reminded me a little of a slice of wet ham straight from the packet.

A gong sounded and I tightened the towel as I rushed to the intercom. I didn't have any idea how to use it and I didn't want to accidentally unlock the door, so I just shouted. "Who is it?"

"It's Atina." There was brief, confused silence. "Can't you see me?"

"I don't know how to use this thing. Hang on a moment!"

Earlier, I'd simply opened the door, but I'd been dressed then. Now I wore nothing but a towel too thin to trust that it would stay in place. I didn't want to accidentally end up naked in front of Atina before we'd even been on our first proper date. Even though most people didn't expect me to be, I was a romantic at heart. I didn't know why everyone assumed that just because I worked on a farm that meant that I couldn't be feminine and romantic. I wanted nothing more than someone who would bring me flowers, chocolates, take me to nice places, make me laugh and listen to me cry, accept all my little weirdnesses and my sheep, talk with-

The towel slipped down my body. And this was exactly why I hadn't opened the door.

"Give me a few minutes!" I shouted, hoping Atina could hear me.

I rummaged for some fresh clothes and quickly threw them on. My hair was a wet mess, so I wrangled it into a ponytail. The alien showers had a setting to dry hair instantaneously, but I didn't like the scratchy feeling it left on my scalp. Sometimes, the old-fashioned way was better than every technology the Kyvens could come up with.

With a quick glance in the mirror to make sure I was more or less presentable, I opened the door. Atina leaned casually against the frame, grinning at me. I couldn't help but smile back.

"Do you want me to explain how the video doorbell works?" she asked helpfully. I was glad she wasn't teasing me for my lack of knowledge.

"Maybe later. Right now, I'm starving. Our meal feels like ages ago already."

"You're right. Herding is an exhausting job. How do you do this all day?"

"To be fair, I don't have to run after the sheep very often. I've trained them well, so now they come when I call for them, or at least when they hear the sound of their feed bucket. I still occasionally have to search for a lost sheep or a lamb that explored too far from the herd, but most of my time is spent making sure they have everything they need. Sometimes, I just sit on the grass and snuggle with the most sociable sheep. Those are the moments when I really love my job."

"I love moments like that. For me, it's when I get to execute a particular challenging manoeuvre and then get that sense of achievement paired with a beautiful view of a planet or a nebula. It's when I remember why I became a pilot in the first place."

"Yes!" I exclaimed passionately before lowering my voice a little. "I always feel sorry for people who don't enjoy their jobs. Being a shepherd isn't exactly glamorous and it certainly doesn't pay much, but it makes me happy. That's what counts."

"What are you counting?"

I opened my mouth to explain that this was yet another idiom when Atina laughed.

"I'm just teasing you. We use the same expression."

"That's fun. We've finally found one that we both know."

We grinned at each other. It felt so natural to talk to Atina, like we'd known each other for much longer than just a few days.

"Let's get some snacks," the pilot suggested. "I have some in my cabin, if you don't fancy the standard meals from the lounge?"

She was inviting me into her cabin. Was there an underlying reason for that or simply because she stored her snacks there? Was this going to end in more than just us having a meal?

Maybe I was overthinking things. Atina had seen how I hadn't been impressed by the ship guts from the food hatch, so here she was being nice and offering to share her snacks.

"Is something wrong?" she asked when I didn't respond right away.

"No, sorry. Abby and Sahra invited me to dinner in their cabin, so I shouldn't eat too much now. What time is it anyway? I took off my controlband when I had a shower and forgot to put it back on."

"I do that all the time! And you still have a while until dinner. Days are longer here on the ship than they are on Kyven, which is why we usually have at least four main meals a day. Did nobody tell you?"

I shook my head. "No, they must have forgotten about that."

"How about I tell you everything you need to know about life on the PoTA-2 while we nibble on some crica crisps?"

She led me away before I could protest and overthink again.

12

ATINA

Jiji was sitting on my bed, honking in excitement that I'd brought Heather with me. The little qoark really seemed to like the human female. I understood why. I'd taken my shower in record time just so I could return to Heather's cabin and spend more time with her. Unfortunately, I had to go back to work soon. My next shift started in less than an hour. Even though we were still stuck on this planet, the captain had assigned a rota for someone to be on the bridge at all times.

I kicked some rubbish to the side. I should've tidied before inviting someone here, unless Heather's species enjoyed being surrounded by mess. I wasn't entirely sure. There was a lot I didn't know about the aliens living on Planet #47283 but I was eager to find out more.

Jiji completely ignored me and bounced up against Heather's feet, begging to be picked up. She was lucky that Heather obliged with a crooked smile that lit her whole face up and made her eyes sparkle. She was really pretty and I found her five fingers and a pinkish complexion, that made her look slightly poisonous according to Kyven standards, endearing.

"You're so fluffy," Heather cooed, discovering how much Jiji liked being thrown up in the air.

My qoark shrieked in delight as it soared up and down and Heather laughed in return. They were so cute together.

I caught myself staring at them like a creep and got some crica chips from my secret stash as promised. "Here."

Heather took a packet, our fingers brushing together. She held my gaze and smiled, a warm smile that felt like a sunrise. "Thanks. If I'd known how bad the food would be, I'd have brought my own snacks. And here I thought airplane food was bad."

"What's an airplane?"

"Oh, umm... Kind of like a spaceship but it doesn't actually travel to space. Just from city to city," Heather replied. "It's made of metal and it flies but don't ask me how it works. Science was never my thing. To be fair, school wasn't my thing. Do you have school in Kyven?"

"Ah, education. Yeah, I didn't like that either. That's why I became a pilot. I have all the freedom in the universe, I get to see cool places, and no responsibilities beyond making sure everyone arrives safely at their destination." I said it with a smile, as always ignoring the hollow ache in my chest. It was great having a life with no dependents or attachments, where I could do as I pleased. I loved it, most of the time. But every now and then, the idea of having somewhere to call home and someone to come home to didn't sound so bad.

Heather gave me a smile that didn't reach her pretty eyes. "I can't say I relate. I loved having the farm, a place that was my own, having animals to take care of that needed me. Even my silly cousin who doesn't need me anymore, the reason why we moved to Kyven."

"You don't like it on Kyven?"

She shook her head. "Kyven is great. I still have my animals, a farm of sorts, but it feels like a weird replica of my old life. There's no banks chasing me for money, so that's great, but there's also nobody to buy wool or eggs or milk... No purpose. Just me and the animals and routine." There was a deep-rooted sadness in her voice that echoed some of the feelings I could never put into words.

I ate a few crisps, enjoying the way they crackled and exploded in my mouth before deflating into a soft powder. "Is that why you're travelling home?"

"Oh, I'm not travelling home." Heather ran a hand through her long hair, tussling the tresses "Huh, I hadn't realised I didn't consider Earth my home anymore, but it's not. I don't have anything there, anyone there. I'm just picking up supplies and then back to... somewhere that's not quite home either."

I touched her shoulder, hoping that would translate as a reassuring gesture and not a weird flirtation or something creepy. This was not the right time for that.

Jiji screamed bloody murder and hissed at me.

"Hey, that's rude. Heather is not a toy to hoard," I told it in my sternest voice, plucking the qoark off of her and putting it on my bed despite its loud protest. "Hey, don't be like that. No, you don't make the rules. I make the rules. I make the— you're not listening to me. I know you don't have ears but I know you can hear me."

Next to me, Heather released a chuckle. "Jiji reminds me of Timo. He can be a little possessive as well."

I racked my brain. "That's your caca, right?"

She snorted. "Cat, and yes. He hisses at me as well if I move him from his sun spot or if I don't give him enough treats. He's quite a peculiar creature but I love him."

My controlband chimed and a little holograph of Captain Ellabee popped up. "Atina, come to the bridge, stat."

I knew that tone, it meant if she had to ask me twice, it would come with an official warning and a deduction in my pay cheque.

"I have to go. My shift is starting." I grimaced at Heather. "Sorry."

She smiled. "No worries, I should probably stop hogging all your time."

"Hogging..."

"Taking up your time," she clarified with that same adorable smile she always had whenever I didn't understand something.

I tried to tickle Jiji. "I'll be back soon."

The qoark turned its backside to me. No cuddles for me tonight then.

Heather chuckled. "Jiji would get on with Timothy. We should go, your captain sounded urgent."

"Yeah, Captain Ellabee is no joke." I held the door of my cabin open for her. "After you."

"Oh, that's a thing for Kyvens as well." Heather's eyes shimmered. "That's nice, I like that. Can I see you after your shift?"

A warmth grew in my chest. "Yes. I'll come find you."

We parted ways and I was still humming and buzzing as I made my way to the bridge where Captain Ellabee was standing over the control panel. "Let's prepare for take-off."

I frowned. "Take-off? I thought we were going to be stuck for a while."

"We got lucky, another ship landed and one of their technician's took a look. Turns out it's not the ship, it's Lini and Inil. They're sick and causing electrical malfunctions and sending scrambled data into the system. I've unplugged them from the mainframe so we'll have to fly the rest of the way manually until I can hire new support. It's going to cost me a rakking fortune but hey, it's worth it not being stuck here. There's nothing here and the food here gives me the..." she shuddered visibly. "Anyway, find Katak and check the ship. We're not staying here any longer than we need to. Oh, and I'm turning stasis on so I don't have to deal with the hungry rashipis. I'm putting the passengers under as well, I don't want any more problems until we arrive at our destination."

Katak joined us, breathing hard. He must have ran to get here. "What's the emergency?"

Captain Ellabee frowned at him. "There is no emergency."

"Does that mean I ran here for nothing?"

I suppressed a laugh at his indignant expression.

Ellabee stayed cool and professional as always. "I was just telling Atina that we're about to take off. I want you to inform the passengers that the ship is going into stasis mode for the rest of the journey. We're behind schedule already and we'll be able to catch up that way."

"I'll inform the passengers," I said quickly. "Katak can do the launch preparations."

The captain's lips quivered into a wry smile. She'd seen Heather and me at the restaurant, so she had to be aware that there was something building between us. I wasn't quite sure yet what it was or even what it could grow into, but I was glad she didn't tell me not to get involved with a passenger.

"Alright. But get back here as soon as possible. If we have another mishap with the ship, I want my two best pilots ready to deal with it."

"Aye, aye, Captain," Katak and I both said at once, before he hurried to his cockpit. I turned to head back the way I'd come, back to Heather.

13

HEATHER

I knew something was wrong when Atina knocked on the door of Abby and Sarah's cabin. After the pilot had left for the bridge, I'd decided to see if they wanted to spend some time with me before our planned dinner. I didn't feel like sitting in my cabin all on my own. Sahra had just pulled out a Kyven board game when Atina arrived.

"There's been a change of plans," the pilot announced. While her words were clearly directed at all of us, I was pleased that she only seemed to have eyes for me. "Captain Ellabee has decided to put the ship into stasis mode. The rashipi escape was the last ring on her ear. She doesn't want anything like this to happen again, especially since we're behind schedule already."

"Last ring on her ear, is that like the last drop in the barrel?" Abby asked her mate.

"Yes, have I not used that expression before?"

They both made gooey eyes at each other and I turned away, focusing on Atina instead. "What does stasis mode mean?"

"The entire ship, bar the bridge, will be frozen in time. Well, technically time will still flow, just very, very slowly. To you, it'll feel like sleeping. When you wake up, we'll be in orbit around your planet. Stasis mode lets us travel much faster, plus there won't be a risk of escaping cargo."

Abby shrugged, apparently not fazed at all. "Guess we won't be having dinner after all. We shall have our next meal on Earth. How does this work, do we lie in our beds?"

"Yes," Atina nodded. "It will be the most comfortable for you. Just lie down and relax. The captain will do a short audio broadcast just before engaging stasis mode, so you won't be surprised by it. I have to go and prepare the rashipis now."

"Can I come with you?" I asked quickly.

"No, you should go to your cabin and get ready," Atina said not unkindly. "I will stay awake while on the bridge, so it's my job to make sure everyone's prepared for stasis."

"But..."

I didn't want to voice my fears in front of Abby and Sahra, who clearly didn't have any issues with the concept of being put to sleep.

"I will take you to your cabin," Atina suggested. "Help you get settled in."

Next to me, Abby chuckled, but I ignored her.

Atina accompanied me to my own room. We stood there, our bodies close simply because the cabin was so small, without saying anything for a while. I didn't want to go to bed. My heart was racing at the thought.

"What's the problem?" Atina asked eventually. "You seem troubled."

I ran a hand through my hair before realising I was even doing it. I clenched my hands together to stop me from fidgeting.

"My father... he passed away during an operation. He was put to sleep and never woke up. I've been terrified of the same thing happening to me or someone I love ever since."

Her expression softened and she reached out, pulling me into her arms. I let her. She was warm and gentle, her hug exactly what I needed.

"I won't let that happen to you," she whispered. "Stasis mode is completely safe. I would love to stay and hold your hand while you fall asleep, but I'm needed on the bridge. However, I promise to be here when you wake up. Deal?"

My anxiety was still making my insides clench with irrational fear, but knowing that she understood helped a little.

"Do you want me to give you something to relax you?"

I shook my head. "No, I'll be fine. I just don't have to like it."

Atina laughed quietly. "No, you don't have to like it. Some people detest stasis mode, but I know why the Captain made the decision to use it for this trip. It will be alright. You might even have some lovely dreams. I've had some of my most beautiful dream adventures during stasis mode."

"And you'll be here when I wake up?" I asked, my voice quivering slightly. I hated feeling so needy.

"I will be. I swear it."

For a moment, I imagined her kneeling next to my sleeping body, leaning down to kiss me awake like the prince in the fairy tale. Maybe I could dream about that. Yes, that would be nice.

Hesitantly, I glanced at the pod that was my bed. I preferred sleeping with the lid open but I had a funny feeling that wasn't going to be possible.

An alarm sounded from Atina's controlband around her wrist and she gave me a sheepish look. "It's time."

With a nod, I discarded my sweater. If I was going to be asleep for who knew how long, I wanted to be comfortable and this weird Kyven material was restrictive.

"Guess I'm going in," I said as I climbed into the bed.

Atina stood over me, a hand resting on top of the lid. "I can come check on you, if you want."

"I'd like that. If I die, promise me you'll tell my

cousin personally." It was silly to worry about something like this when most likely, nothing bad would happen, but I didn't like the idea of being put to sleep artificially. I'd seen plenty of creepy stories about cryosleep and that kind of thing in movies. I'd always thought all of that was made up but maybe they were written by people like me who had gone into outer space too.

The beautiful pilot knelt down next to me. "I will but you shouldn't worry. Stasis is super safe, even for your species."

"I hope so. When I wake up, we'll be on Earth?"

"Nearing it," she confirmed with a nod.

"That's kind of neat." I tried to focus on that part and how lovely it would be to see familiar sights again. I could eat pizza, and haggis, and a deep-fried mars bars, even if they were vile.

Atina smiled reassuringly. "You're going to be fine. Maybe when we're on... Earth? Is that what you call it?"

I nod.

"Isn't that the same word for dirt?"

I chuckled. "It is. What does Kyven mean?"

"It..." She went silent, thinking for a moment. "It means blue."

"Not very original either," I teased, feeling ever so slightly less nervous. "You were saying?"

"Oh, when we're on Earth, maybe you could show me around? I've never been and I'm curious."

I briefly took her hand in mine, drawing a lot of strength from just her touch. "I'd like that a lot."

A loud voice boomed through the cabin. "Activating stasis momentarily, all passengers and non-essential crew must take residence in their assigned pods."

Atina smiled. "That's you."

I nodded and lied down, my head nicely on the middle of my pillow. "Do I need to count sheep?"

Confusion marred Atina's face, a lovely last image before the lid of the pod descended on me, trapping me in what felt like eternal darkness. In the vague distance, I heard the chime of my cabin door opening and closing which meant Atina was gone and I was all alone.

I reached up, testing if the lid of the pod would open.

It wouldn't.

Kind of like a coffin.

A hint of panic rushed through me and my breathing echoed through my ears as I tried to stay calm. Everything was going to be fine. And if it wasn't fine... at least I had my parents waiting for me on the other side. Would they be disappointed that I left Rachel behind or would they be happy to see me again after all those years?

I wasn't sure.

Something hummed and my eyelids grew heavy. I struggled to keep them open, fighting for one more moment of consciousness before I sank into a deep sleep, dreaming of pink fluff balls, alien sheep, and Atina's wonderful green eyes.

14

ATINA

Flying through space undisturbed was usually my favourite bit but I kind of missed Heather's company and all of the funny things she said and asked.

I counted down, keeping a close eye on the map as we neared the orbit of her planet. According to the speed we were currently going at, it wouldn't be long until we'd have to turn on the deflection shields so we could land without being detected.

"I'm starving," Katak complained loudly from the other side of the bridge.

Captain Ellabee sighed. "Then get some more ship guts."

"I'm sick and tired of guts. Did we really have to put the cook and all the kitchen staff in stasis?"

"Yes," the captain said firmly. "But we'll wake them

soon enough. We're almost there, look." She pointed at a rapidly nearing blue dot in the visor.

"That's Earth?" I asked.

"If our maps are to be trusted." She called a holoscreen from her controlband. "Seven more clicks until we're there. Get ready to fly manually and start preparing for landing."

"When are we lifting stasis?" I asked, eager for Heather to wake up again. Since she'd gone into stasis, I'd read up on her planet and I had so many questions.

"We'll lift it when we've landed. I don't need any distractions or interruptions," the captain said in a voice that made it clear this wasn't a discussion. She stretched her arms and groaned. "Since Lini and Inil aren't here for support, let's be extra careful. I want a soft landing."

Katak glanced at me before he spoke. "Are you sure?"

The Captain nodded. "I don't need another accident. I don't think they have repair ports on this planet, so if the ship breaks down, we'll have to call for assistance and we could be stranded there for a good while."

That didn't sound that bad to me. I'd have Heather's company. That being said, if I let the ship crash, I'd be out of a job and probably, my bowels.

My gut twisted just thinking about a disembowelment and I focused my attention back on my control panel. The blue planet was nearing at extreme speeds and growing bigger and bigger with every moment. Blobs of green and brown were making itself known, with wisps of white throughout. It was quite pretty, especially because of how much blue there was.

It made me wonder if everyone on this planet was Heather's colour or if there would be some people with my skin tone too.

"Nearing Planet #47283's orbit," Katak announced.

"Heard. Let's take her off autopilot," I replied, strapping myself in properly and reaching for the switch. "On my count."

"I'm with you," Katak said.

"Great. In three, two, one," I counted, flicking the switch off at the same time as my co-pilot. A green light came on.

"*Autopilot off,*" a robotic voice said.

A thrill shot through me from having the ship in hands and knowing that one bad movement could lead to a disaster. It was a lot of power, responsibility, and one of the best parts of flying. It was certainly when I felt the most free.

Our external scanners showed a few small objects orbiting the planet, but no other ships. I instructed the AI to scan on a few more frequencies to detect any hidden vessels just in case. I was used to hundreds, if not thousands of spaceships circling Kyven, so not having any show up on my screen made me suspicious.

"How advanced is this planet?" I asked Captain Ellabee without turning away from my screens.

"Not very. They've barely reached their own moon.

It'll be a long time until they're able to reach Kyven, let alone other planets even further away."

"Cute."

The captain chuckled. "Which is why we don't want to be spotted by the natives, so concentrate on your job. Are the shields up yet?"

"Of course. We wouldn't even show up on modern scanners, let alone whatever they rely on."

"Good. Katak, are you ready as well?"

"Aye, Captain. Waiting for your command to enter orbit."

We went through the motions, a well-practised team. I loved this part of my job. The thrill of flying manually paired with seeing a new planet for the first time. Planet 47283 didn't look dissimilar to Kyven, except that it was a little smaller and had a lot more water covering its surface. I couldn't wait to see what it looked like from down below.

"I've located a suitable landing location close to our destination," Katak reported. "Sending coordinates to Atina now."

By now, I trusted the other pilot enough that I didn't double-check his coordinates. If he said the location was big enough for the PoTA-2 to land, it was good enough for me.

When the heat shields around us began to glow in a tell-tale red, I couldn't help but grin with excitement. We were getting closer to landing, that moment when I got a healthy rush of adrenaline and felt like I'd succeeded at my task. Flying was great, landing safely was even better.

The location Katak had chosen was on the outskirts of a settlement. Rivers crossed the landscape as blue lines, intersected by grey-black lines covered in tiny colourful spots. Vehicles, maybe, that weren't set up to fly. How idyllic and old-fashioned. Maybe Heather could take me for a ride in one.

I had to evade one large flying object, but it was slow despite its size and easy to outmanoeuvre. Was this the *plane* that Heather had mentioned?

"Engaging landing gear," I said automatically when the prompt appeared on my screen. "Two hundred lengths to the ground. Prepare for landing."

Usually, Captain Ellabee would have given a command via the intercom at this stage, but with almost everyone in stasis, all of the crew awake were already on the bridge.

I did the last few pre-landing checks before taking a deep breath. It was part of my ritual that had become a habit ever since learning the ropes at flight school.

"Landing in five...four...three...breaks engaged...and we've arrived."

The PoTA-2 barely swerved when we touched down on solid ground. This was a textbook landing, so much better than the shuttle landing on Kyven.

"Nice one," Captain Ellabee praised. "Let's do all the necessary checks first before we reverse the stasis mode. I'm rather enjoying the peace and quiet."

As much as I was looking forward to spending more

time with Heather again, I couldn't help but agree with Ellabee. The atmosphere on the bridge was a lot more relaxed with only a skeleton crew present. Plus there was no chance of the rashipis escaping again while they were asleep.

I went through the motions until the captain was satisfied that no locals would be able to stumble across the PoTA-2 by accident. If anyone got too close to the perimeter I'd drawn, they'd suddenly feel the urge to return home. It was a very useful piece of technology that Ellabee had paid quite a lot for, but it enabled us to land on planets that didn't have an official spaceport yet. Loading cargo was much easier this way than having to use a shuttle.

"Now go and wake your human," Ellabee said with a suggestive grin. "I know you've been waiting for it."

"I...Thanks."

I didn't even bother denying it. For once, the captain didn't seem to care that relationships between crew and passengers were against the rules. She was unpredictable that way. Going against some of her rules could easily result in disembowelment, while breaking others didn't have any consequences at all.

I rushed to Heather's cabin, arriving just in time to hear the signal that stasis mode was about to be turned off. I opened Heather's pod and waited patiently for her to wake up. She looked beautiful in her sleep, so calm and serene that I was tempted to stroke her cheek. But I resisted. She wasn't awake yet. If I'd misread all her signals, I didn't want to breach her boundaries.

Finally, her eyelids fluttered open. I made sure that I was in her line of vision so that I'd be the first thing she saw. She yawned widely, then smiled when she became awake enough to recognise me.

"You."

"Me." I grinned. "Did you sleep well?"

"Mmmhm. I think I dreamed... no, I can't remember. But it feels like it was a nice dream. Are we near Earth now?"

"We've already landed. The captain thought it would be a good idea to wait until after the landing to lift stasis mode. We have three planetary days now until lift off. Do you want to show me around? Jiji is staying here, Katak will be keeping it company. I don't have a LightScreen ring small enough for the qoark."

She sat up with another yawn. "Do you know where we are? If we've landed somewhere outside the UK, I doubt I'll be able to be a good guide. I've never travelled much myself. It's hard to go on holiday when you have a farm to look after."

I opened a holo map on my controlband and showed her our current location.

"Oh, the Yorkshire Dales, that's the middle of nowhere! Why did you choose to land here?"

"Katak said it was close to our destination, but I didn't ask how close. Maybe he got something mixed up. Is this anywhere near your home?"

"No, and it's not near any major city either for us to get supplies! Abby wants to visit her parents, but I'm not sure where they live. I suppose they'll have to go to

Leeds and take a train from there, but how will we even get there? It's not like we have a car."

"We have a shuttle with camouflage mode," I explained. "It will take on the form of a local transportation vehicle to blend in. It works similarly to LightScreen technology that we use to look like the natives. If your vehicles don't fly, the shuttle will convert to ground-transportation as well."

"How handy." Heather's face lit up. "Can I decide what vehicle it turns into? I've always wanted to drive a Mini."

I chuckled. "Let's find out."

15

HEATHER

I was jittery with nerves as I waited for the ramp to open and I wrung my hands together in an attempt to avoid chewing my lip.

Next to me, Abby caught my eye and offered a smile. "Nervous?"

I nodded, not trusting my voice to speak. I'd seen the date on the controlband when we landed. Iit had been over a year since Tamsia landed on our farm and willingly abducted us, and I was worried, curious, and excited to find out what had changed so far.

Maybe nothing. Maybe everything.

A lot could happen in a year.

The door hissed open and fresh air rushed into the spaceship, carrying the smell of dirt, grass, and rain. It wasn't quite the same as a farm but it was a proper

British smell. I hadn't realised how much I missed it until it filled my lungs.

I stepped off the metal ramp and onto the swampy grass of the Dales. It squelched. "I wish I brought my wellies."

Abby chuckled. "We really are in the middle of nowhere."

"Atina said we landed in the Yorkshire Dales." I took in the landscape, admiring the view. It was gorgeous. Chilly, with long grey clouds that looked like they could release rain on us any moment. Exactly how I remembered it.

"Did someone say my name?" a light voice said next to me.

I turned, my eyes widening. Atina's usual gorgeous blue skin was now a bright pink that reminded me of a lawn flamingo.

Abby tactfully muffled her snort. I didn't quite manage the same.

"What's going on here?" I asked, gesturing to all of Atina.

"I'm testing out the LightScreen technology," she explained, twisting a ring around her finger that returned her to her normal blue and back which coloured her a shade down of fuchsia.

"I think you might have put the wrong values in," Abby said sweetly. "Sahra uses $X12GB$ and that does a good job counteracting her blue."

Atina fiddled with the ring and the obnoxious pink settled to a much paler shade. Her beautiful green hair was now a dull dark blonde but her sparkling eyes had retained their original colour. She was still gorgeous, though, and her bright smile was unchanged.

I took her hand in mine and gave it a light squeeze. It didn't matter to me what she looked like.

A wide grin brightened her face and she gestured behind her. "The shuttle is being undocked on the other side. It's set to take us to the nearest city. Leids."

"Leeds," I corrected gently as I followed her around the spaceship where a standard white van was waiting for us. It had number plates and everything, including a bumper sticker and a little flag on the radio antenna. It was hard to believe this was an illusion. It was only on closer inspection that I noticed the vehicle was ever so slightly hovering.

Atina pulled the side door open. "All aboard."

I climbed in first, with Abby right behind me. Sahra joined a moment later, taking a seat next to her girlfriend.

The inside of the van was bright and large enough to stand upright in. I could also see through all the walls, which was both amazing and scary. I reached out, relieved when my hand bumped against an invisible barrier.

At least there was no risk of falling out.

I smiled at Abby and Sahra. I couldn't say we'd become friends but we were definitely on much friendlier terms than when we left. "You said you wanted to visit your parents, right? Do they live in Chester as well?" I asked.

"No, I'll have to hop on a train." Abby's face scrunched up. "One thing I haven't missed, public transport."

I chuckled. "Can't say I have either. I'm trying to figure out if I'll have enough time to go up to the farm."

"Ah, feeling a little homesick?" Abby asked.

"I'm not sure yet," I told her honestly. "I feel like I'm trapped in between places. This used to be my home, but it no longer feels this way. Nor does Kyven. I like it there, I like the people, I like having my cousin close by, but when I think of home, Kyven isn't it."

Abby nodded, but it was clear that she didn't share my sentiments. She'd found both a home and a mate on Kyven.

Atina slid onto the seat on my other side and strapped herself in. She'd fumbled with the shuttle's controls until now, but from the way she looked at me with true sympathy, she'd clearly listened to our conversation. "I understand. I looked for a home for a long time until I found it."

I looked at her curiously. "You found it?"

Atina smiled, contentment mirrored on her no-longer-blue face. "Space is my home. I never feel as much at home as when I'm in the cockpit, steering the PoTA-2 from one exciting planet to the next. Partly it's the freedom, partly the crew. I know some people prefer to have a house on solid ground, but I wouldn't exchange my little cabin on Captain Ellabee's ship for any building in the universe."

Her eyes blazed with passion. I almost felt jealous

of her certainty. Once, I'd felt like that about my farm, my sheep, but that had all changed. Would I ever find that feeling of being home again or was I going to feel out of place for the rest of my life?

"Maybe going to the farm will help me draw a line under that part of my life," I said slowly. "And I know all the suppliers in that area. We can get everything we need there, probably for better prices than in the big city. Only question is how long it'll take to get there from here. It's a beautiful part of the country, but I really don't understand why your colleague chose to land here."

The shuttle began to move, although if I hadn't seen the scenery move past us, I wouldn't have known. There was no rumble, no sound, not even the slightest tremor beneath my feet. I hoped we wouldn't run over a poor pedestrian who didn't hear us coming once we got into more populated areas.

"I've set the ground shuttle's speed to emulate that of your planet's standard vehicles. It could go a lot faster, but we don't want to draw attention."

"I like this speed," Abby said, suddenly sounding a little queasy. "But I don't think I'd get used to travelling this way. Seeing the landscape move without any barrier between me and outside is...unsettling."

Sahra squeezed her mate's hand. The Kyven was watching our surroundings with wide eyes, taking everything in. She'd been to Earth before, but I didn't think she'd seen a place as breathtaking as the Dales with their rolling hills, ancient stone walls and endless green fields.

"I can make the shuttle walls visible," Atina offered helpfully.

I wished she hadn't. As soon as the walls around us turned into bronze metal without a single window, I felt sleepy. I'd just been in stasis for who knew how long, but I had trouble keeping my eyes open. If we were travelling at the speed of a normal car, we'd be travelling for at least another two hours. Enough time for a nap. I closed my eyes and let myself drift off, comfortably aware of Atina's calm presence next to me.

16

ATINA

Heather's head rested on my shoulder as I watched her sleep. She didn't even wake when we dropped off Sahra and Abby in Leeds, arranging to pick them up again on the way back to the PoTA-2. Both females looked tired as well; a side effect of the stasis. I on the other hand was wide awake. I'd turned the shuttle walls translucent again as soon as they'd left, marvelling at this planet's strange beauty. The area we were driving through now was less wild than the green hills where we'd landed, but it was still fascinating. All around us, humans drove in their primitive four-wheeled vehicles, their hands at the wheel. They hadn't even invented driverless ground shuttles yet. How were they supposed to have a proper conversation - or a relaxing nap - if they had to stay in control of the vehicle?

I checked the dashboard with the coordinates Heather had given me of her farm. Part of me, selfishly, hoped she wouldn't want to stay. This planet was pretty enough but not very advanced. The colours and primitive structures were cute. There was lots of meadow though, more and more as the shuttle followed the route.

Heather stirred and murmured the cutest noise as she woke up from her slumber. I still found it weird how her species willingly went into an unconscious state but apparently, that was normal for them.

"Hey," she said, yawning. "Where are we?"

"Umm." I checked the coordinates. "We're about fifteen of your... minutes away from our destination."

Heather sat up and glanced out through the window, commenting on the passing landscape. "Ah, yes, I recognise where we are. Oh, these houses are new. What a random place for a new-build. No! The Pig And Swan is closing down? That's a shame, they make the best homemade chips."

"What are chips?" I asked.

"Fried potato wedges. They're fluffy on the inside, crispy on the outside, and bad for the waistline." She patted her tummy. "But so worth it. We'll get you some, they're a must try. Oh, and tea. And cheese. I miss cheese. And cupcakes. You know what, let's just stop at the nearest supermarket."

I nodded. "Great. What's a supermarket?"

"Oh, this is fun. I'm not the one who knows nothing anymore." A big grin tugged Heather's lips up. "Oh, go left here. That's the way to the farm. Careful, the road is quite narrow."

"Got it." I took manual control over the shuttle so I didn't mow down the local flora. Heather seemed fond of it and it was better not to leave any trace of our presence behind.

A long building came into view and Heather visibly tensed. Her hands balled into fists on top of her knees and she was no longer smiling. This had to be her former home.

I stalled the shuttle next to a similar looking vehicle but much lower and in a bright red colour.

Heather got out without saying anything and I hurried after her, making sure to lock the shuttle so no human could get into our vehicle and get the surprise of their lives.

"Looks like someone else lives here now," Heather said in a sombre tone. "I'm not sure why I thought coming here was a good idea."

I gently touched the small of her back. "You wanted to see your former home. It's understandable."

"It was dumb." Her gaze travelled from the main building to a shed on the side. "They repaired the fence. That's nice. I don't like the blue paint but I guess it's lively."

I stayed quiet, giving her space to look around and take in the changes. It couldn't be easy to come back after all this time and have someone else live here. I felt weird whenever someone entered my cabin or sat in my chair, this had to be incredibly strange for her.

Heather paused in front of a wooden bench in front of a window. "My dad actually made this. It was a present for my mum's birthday because she loved the view. They would sit here every Sunday and have their morning coffee. Rachel and I used to as well, once they passed."

I joined her by the bench. "Do you regret leaving?"

"No, I don't. I'm grateful that Tamsia took us when she did." Heather sat down and sighed sadly.

"How did a Kyven end up here actually?" I asked, carefully sitting down next to her. I felt like I was intruding on a very personal and intimate moment but Heather didn't seem to mind my presence. On the contrary.

She took my hand and rested her head on my shoulder. "It's a long story, but basically, my cousin met Tamsia at a party and made quite an impression on her. When she came to Earth to buy some cows, Tamsia came to our farm, and they fell in love."

"And then you both went with her to Kyven?"

"Yes. We were deep in debt. Do you know what debt is?"

"Oh, I know what that is," I assured her.

"The bank would've taken everything. Luckily, Tamsia offered to take us along. We still lost the farm and the land, but at least we got to keep the animals. And I didn't have to say goodbye to my cousin."

I nodded slowly. "Is it hard being away from her?"

"Yes and no. I love her like a sister but now that she has Tamsia, we've drifted apart. Not in a bad way, just in a natural manner. She has her own life now and I have the animals. I just want... more." Heather sighed. "I thought coming back here might give me some closure or an idea of what I want from my new life, but it's just weird. And I know I suggested we come here, but I'm worried someone will recognise me."

"You could use a LightScreen ring," I suggested. "I have a spare one in the shuttle."

Heather offered me a smile. "No, that's okay. It's not right coming back here as anyone else but myself. And I might still be able to get good deals from the local vendors."

"That makes sense."

She straightened up. "Oh, oh, someone's coming."

Just like she said, another kyvenoid walked up to the farm and paused in front of us. If my research was to be believed, it looked like a male.

He raised his hand. "Can I help you?"

Heather got up from the bench and smiled. "Sorry for intruding. A friend of mine used to live here."

"Oh, you knew the former owners? Do you know what happened to them? We're new in the region but we heard they fell off the face of the Earth," the man said.

"They moved very far away," Heather replied.

I bit back a grin. That was an understatement if there ever was one.

"Are you going to see them again soon?" the man asked. "Or do you have a forwarding address for them?

We found this bundle of letters when we moved in and thought they might like them."

It was clear that Heather was having a hard time trying to pretend that she wasn't extremely keen to find out more.

"Where did you find them?"

"Funny story, actually. We pulled down the wall between the kitchen and living room to give us an open plan layout, and between the bricks was this little metal box. At first we thought it was a time capsule, but when we saw that it contained personal letters we decided not to read them." He laughed heartily. "My wife thinks that reading them might earn us the ire of whatever ghosts live in the farmhouse. The building is old, you see, and she's convinced that we have a ghost living in the rafters."

Heather laughed as well, but it didn't reach her eyes. "More likely for that to be rats."

"I agree, but don't tell my wife. Anyway, want me to get those letters for you? It would be lovely to know that they're back with the family who owned this place."

"I will make sure they get them." Her voice quivered slightly. "Thank you for being so thoughtful."

The male kyvenoid walked back to the house with a wave, giving us the chance to talk openly.

"Did you know about these letters?" I asked Heather.

"No, I had no idea. I wonder who they belonged to. My grandfather built this farm, but I know that my parents extended the house just after they married, so it could be either of them. Or maybe someone else entirely, a builder who left them as a joke? I can't wait to read them."

I squeezed her hand, earning myself a smile that this time extended to her beautiful eyes.

"Are you glad now that we came here?"

"Yes, maybe it was meant to be. But as soon as he returns with the letters I think we should go. Seeing the farm again makes me all emotional. Shopping for supplies will take my mind off things. Retail therapy always works."

"Retail therapy," I echoed. "I like that expression. I'm going to use that from now on."

The man stepped out of the building, now carrying a large woven basket. Behind him, a female poked her head out of the door to look at us. She waved enthusiastically, but didn't join her mate by the fence. Heather raised her hand in response and I copied her.

"Sorry, my wife is on the phone or she would have said hello properly," he huffed, out of breath. "I've added some of our produce as a little gift. We really love this place and still can't believe our luck to have found it. We were looking for a farm like this for ages and had almost given up hope. It's our own little paradise, so please tell the previous owners that we appreciate them taking such great care of the land."

Heather squeezed my hand tightly as she struggled to keep her composure. "I will let them know. Thank you very much for keeping the letters. Most people would have thrown them away or given them to a museum. I know my friend will appreciate it."

"Not a problem. Now I better get back to my sheep, one of the ewe's close to lambing. It was good to meet you!"

"Good to meet you, too," Heather muttered, her attention on the letters.

I pulled her back towards the shuttle. "Let's look at them somewhere private."

17

HEATHER

Of all the things I'd expected to happen during our visit to Earth, this wasn't it. As soon as the fake van's doors closed behind us, I sat down the basket and rummaged through its contents. A jar of honey, an assortment of jams, a ball of hand-dyed wool and a little bottle of mead. The new owners must have introduced bees to the farm. I almost felt jealous for a moment, then remembered that I would have lost the farm either way. Moving to Kyven had been a much better option than becoming bankrupt and trying to survive here without a penny to my name.

The last item in the basket was a small bundle wrapped in an embroidered tea towel. I impatiently undid the string tied around it, my fingers shaking ever so slightly. Inside was a stack of a dozen or so yellowed envelopes. The paper was so old that it was stiff and frail beneath my touch. I carefully opened the top envelope and pulled out a folded piece of paper. The ink had faded in places, making it hard to read, but I managed to decipher the name at the very end. Tristan. My grandfather. I didn't remember much of him besides his wild beard that I used to pull on as a toddler when he carried me in his arms. He'd passed away when I was four, so all I knew about him were the stories my parents had told.

I scanned the top of the letter. Dearest Elise. Granny. A warm, fuzzy feeling spread through my belly. She'd been my favourite grandparent, always up for a laugh, a cuddle or a hearty meal.

The next letter I pulled from the stack was in much better condition. The old-fashioned handwriting was beautiful but also not the easiest to read.

My dearest Tristan,

I cannot express how much joy your last letter brought me.

Hearing that you are not only alive, but returning soon, brightened my day. I will prepare your favourite sourdough bread for your arrival and wear the red dress you like so much.

All my love,

Your Elise.

I smiled at the beautiful note, letting my fingers brush over the old paper. It was such a lovely note and so sweet that grandfather brought these back from the war with him. They were probably a lifeline while he was deep in the trenches.

"Rachel will love these," I said, carefully tucking the letter back in the envelope and just sitting with the letters. "It was really hard when Granny passed. We were all really close. My dad was devastated but he said it helped him to imagine she was in a better place. That's what I told myself when they passed, that they were all in a better place. It took me a long while to get used to the quiet."

Atina gave me a sad smile. "I know how you feel. My parents astralised when I was young. That's how I got into piloting. It was good to have something to do, somewhere to belong. The rush keeps me distracted but sometimes it can get lonely onboard." The other woman twisted her LightScreen ring, returning to her normal blue colour. "The crew is my family now. Some days, I still feel lonely, but I'm no longer alone."

"I get it. Being alone is weird. Lonely is awful, but alone is just... a different beast."

"But you're not alone, you have your cousin, and now me."

I gulped, my heartbeat quickening. "You're sweet."

She took my hand in hers and gave it a gentle squeeze. "Do you want to look around more?"

My gaze travelled to the farm and I shook my head. "No, I think I want to go. It was lovely to be back and know it's in good hands, but it's no longer my home."

Atina nodded. "I understand. Time for retail-therapy?"

"Yes, please. Hang on, just a moment." I hopped out of the van and dashed to the bench, half-bent over so I wasn't visible through the window. The farmer seemed lovely and kind but I didn't want to risk them seeing me.

I waved at Atina. "Come give me a hand."

She frowned as she came over, mimicking my run and looking adorable as she did. "What are we doing?"

"We're taking the bench. It's my parents' bench." I glanced in the window, reassured that nobody was looking, and picked up one end. "Okay, go, go, go."

Atina laughed, a wonderful bubbly sound as we hauled the old bench into the shuttle. I heard stumbling in the farm but kept running. It didn't matter if they called the cops or told on me, I didn't plan on coming back here.

"Drive," I instructed, strapping myself in. "Hurry, hurry."

The shuttle set in motion and we pulled away. A strange calm came over me as the farm grew smaller and smaller and eventually disappeared when we went over the green hill. I thought it would be harder to be back but it just enforced the feeling that this place was no longer home.

"Let's park at the church," I instructed, pointing at the parking lot. "Then we don't have to pay."

With a nod, Atina did as I asked and parked neatly between the lines.

"Impressive," I told her. "I was never any good at parking."

"I'm not a pilot for nothing," she said with a proud grin, her gaze drifting to the bench. "That's going to be hard to smuggle on the ship. We should make sure the captain doesn't see that."

"Why? Can't we just bring it up with the other supplies?" I asked.

"Oh, right. Yes, that makes sense. See, this is why I could never be a smuggler." Atina gave me a look. "Are you sure you're okay? That must've been weird to be back at your old home."

I nodded. "Yes, I'm okay. It was... cathartic. Do you understand that word?"

"I'm not sure. Is it the same feeling as when I found the Kendari who mistreated Jiji and kicked him right in the gachinks?"

"I don't know what gachinks are but that doesn't sound pleasant," I said, chuckling. "But I'm not sure if that's the same as catharsis. It's more like... relief after a long period of stress, when your insides go all quiet and there's calm inside your heart."

"Ah, I see. On Kyven, we call that Ama'ta."

"Ama'ta," I echoed. "That's a nice word. It reminds me of Ba'ta'k."

Atina gave me a curious look. "You know what Ba'ta'k is?"

"Yes, Rachel and Tamsia are planning theirs. Here, it's called marriage. Kind of. It seems deeper on Kyven, more intense and more binding."

"Marriage." Atina nodded. "I read about that in my research."

"What research?"

"I researched your planet and customs while you were in stasis," Atina said, looking proud of herself. She ran a hand through her lovely green hair. "Marriage is a legal union between two people."

"It is. How come you were reading about marriage?"

Atina's dark blue skin flushed slightly. "I was curious. I also read about mouth kisses"

Her endearing way of wording that made me snort. "It's just called a kiss."

"But that doesn't specify where you're kissing."

"No, but you can usually guess from context." I leaned in and tilted my face slightly. "See, I'm turning my head so I'm clearly going for a kiss on the cheek."

To my surprise, Atina moved closer and pressed her blue lips on my cheek. A little jolt of delight shot through me and I didn't pull away nearly as fast as I thought I would.

Instead, I turned to face her, my voice reduced to a whisper. I inched towards her, nerves tingling through me. "And like this, that's a regular kiss."

Atina moved even closer, pausing in front of me, so close I could feel her warm breath on my lips. "I've never given a mouth kiss before."

She was too cute.

I shuffled closer and brushed the back of my hand over her cheek, marvelling at how soft her skin was and how beautiful her eyes were. I pressed my lips on hers, briefly, a soft kiss that made my whole body tingle. It had been so long since I had any romantic intimacy, it was like someone set a whole bunch of fireworks alight in my stomach.

We broke apart and I sat back. "How was that for you?"

Atina grinned. "That's nice. Is it my turn now?"

"It's not exactly a turn thing, but yes."

She leaned in and pressed her lips on mine, equally as gentle and tender. My heart pounded even more and I parted my lips, inviting Atina in for more. Butterflies fluttered in my chest as she deepened the kiss. Her research had clearly worked.

She was slightly breathless when the kiss ended. "I like that a lot. Does that mean we're mates now?"

My chest constricted. I knew what mate meant to Kyvens. She wasn't just asking me to be her girlfriend, it was a much bigger commitment, one I wasn't sure I could make. I should've considered this before I let myself get closer to the lovely pilot.

I moved back, a chill running down my spine. I shouldn't have kissed her on a whim. "Look, I really like you, Atina. But we live very different lives. You clearly love your ship so I can't ask you to leave it, but I don't know if I can be away from Rachel or my animals all the time."

"Oh." Disappointment filled Atina's deep blue eyes. "I understand."

"Sorry."

"It's okay, I understand." She offered me a smile but the hurt was clear on her face. "So, retail-therapy?" Without waiting for my reply, she got out of the shuttle.

[18]

ATINA

I trailed after Heather while she bought all the things she needed. I didn't know anything about cattle feed, hay, and all the other items Heather needed, so I stayed in the background, letting her do the negotiations. I helped her carry her purchases to the shuttle whenever she needed me to, but we didn't exchange many words.

I could still taste her on my lips. That mouth kiss had been simply amazing. Even more exhilarating than flying through an asteroid field at high speed. I wanted to feel that again. My gaze was drawn to her lips again and again, wondering if she had felt the same way. Had she enjoyed the kiss or had it been nothing special for her? Maybe she did this all the time. That would explain why she'd rejected me so easily.

I'd read up on humans, but I knew from experience

that you couldn't believe everything you read, especially when it came to a barely researched species like humans. Once they left their own solar system, they would become more interesting to other aliens, but right now, there wasn't a whole lot of information on them.

"Atina, are you coming?"

I realised Heather was holding a door open for me. I'd been so deep in thought that I hadn't even looked where I was going. We were on our fifth stop and I was getting bored of retail therapy. Shopping was a lot more fun when it involved items that I actually wanted rather than yet another bale of hay.

"This farm shop has a tea room at the back. I think we've earned ourselves a scone."

"What's a scone?"

"One of the best things ever, you'll see. Come on, I hope they still have some fruit scones left."

She led me through a warren of shelves and boxes until we emerged in an open space at the other end of the building. Five tiny tables were squeezed into the room, one of them unoccupied. Heather steered right towards the empty table while pointing at a counter to our left.

"It looks like they've increased their cake selection since I was last here. You should try some cake. And scones. Mmhm, maybe we can take some with us for later?"

I looked at the plates filled with strange mounds and balls of baked dough. Some of them looked appetising, while with some of them I wasn't even sure if they were food.

As soon as we took a seat, a young female appeared from behind the counter. Her hair was as blue as my own, but set into short spikes. She had silver rings stuck in her nose, ears and bottom lip. I had a lot of questions, but didn't want to ask them while the young human was still in earshot.

"What can I get you?" she asked with an accent that wasn't like Heather's at all. Maybe that was the translator's fault.

"I'll take a darjeeling tea and a fruit scone with clotted cream and jam," Heather said immediately. "And a piece of that Victoria sponge, it was delicious last time I was here."

The young female looked at me questioningly. Without a menu and not knowing what any of the food was, I went for the simplest option. "I'll have what she's having."

The human smiled and left. Just when I was about to ask Heather about the blue hair, her eyes went wide and she seemed to shrink into her seat.

"That's Jack, my former neighbour!" she whispered. "I don't want him to see me."

I turned around to see a bulky male who'd just entered the cafe. His attention was on the food in the counter, but it wouldn't be long until he turned to check for a free table.

Without thinking, I ripped off my LightScreen ring

and handed it to Heather. It would disguise her from the male.

A gasp from behind me made me realise my mistake.

"She's blue!" a female exclaimed.

Someone else shushed her, but the damage was done. Everyone was looking at me. Caca shit. What was I going to do now?

Heather stared at me in shock, her eyes wide. She held the LightScreen ring that I'd thrust at her, but with everyone's eyes on us, neither of us could put it on.

My bowels ached in anticipation of my near-future disembowelment. When Captain Ellabee found out that I'd exposed myself in front of the natives, I'd be lucky to get away without my bowels. She might fire me as well. Rak, rak, rak. This was bad. So bad.

Heather stood up, still staring at me, and began to clap her hands together. When the crowd's attention moved to her, she made a strange whooping sound that the translator didn't interpret for me. A human ritual, maybe?

"Very well done," Heather cheered with fake enthusiasm. "My friend has been practising this trick for months!"

Behind me, someone also started clapping, joined by another person, until everyone patted their hands together. I still had no clue what was going on.

"Bow," Heather hissed beneath her breath.

I bowed my head to her, and when she wiggled her

eyebrows, I stood up and bowed even further down until my nose touched the table.

"How did you do that?" a male asked.

"A magician never reveals her tricks," Heather said quickly before I could come up with a response. "Atina, you might want to go to the toilet and take off your costume?"

She took my hand, giving me my LightScreen ring back without anyone seeing it.

"The toilets are just over here. I'll show you."

Still holding my hand, she dragged me to a door I hadn't noticed before. It had two kyvenoid shapes on it, one with legs, one with a triangle on its bottom half that may have represented a tail.

As soon as the door closed behind us, Heather breathed in deeply. "Wow, that was one way of taking the attention off me. What were you thinking?"

"I wasn't," I admitted dumbly. "I'm sorry, I'm so sorry. I just wanted to make sure that neighbour didn't recognise you and..."

"Oh, shut up."

Her lips crushed on mine.

This was a very different mouth kiss from before. She was rushed, demanding, moving against me with a strange urgency that took hold of me as well. I wrapped my arms around her, pulling her closer. Her tongue nudged against my lips until I opened them for her. She moaned against me while I drowned in her taste, in her warmth. I closed my eyes, focusing on the way she felt.

Familiar tingles rushed through me, ones I usually

only felt when someone caressed my ears in just the right way. That was a gesture only reserved for mates though, which Heather already said she didn't want to be.

Unsure what to make of it, I pulled back. "We're mouth kissing again."

Heather's cheeks took on a lovely rosy colour. "We are. Sorry, this must be confusing."

"A little," I told her, searching her face for any clues or signs. Her expressive eyebrows made that fairly easy usually, but they stayed flat and unmoving. That was hard, that could mean anything.

Heather gave me a sheepish smile and looked away. "Do you think we've waited long enough for the people to have forgotten about us? We might have to leave the cakes behind but I'm not comfortable sitting back down after that spectacle. It's a shame, those are the best bits of an afternoon tea."

I just nodded, guilty that I'd ruined our lovely meal. I clearly made a thoughtless mistake earlier taking my disguise off and I'd be lucky if it didn't end up costing me my bowels or worse, my job. Captain Ellabee was strict when it came to these blunders, especially if someone reported it to the Galactic Union. It could cost her her licence and get her a hefty fine on top as well.

Hopefully, that wouldn't happen. I wasn't entirely sure what Heather said to cover it up and the mouth kiss had distracted me from asking. I put the LightScreen ring back on and twisted it, covering up my blue complexion so I could fit in again. The reflective mirror assured me that I was now looking similar to Heather, even if I barely recognised myself.

We snuck out to the shuttle and Heather seemed relieved when we were inside. "Let's get the hell out of here. We've got everything we came for and you've probably made quite an impression on the locals."

I started the shuttle with the touch of my hand and pulled it towards the grey road. I'd feed it the coordinates of the ship once we were in more open terrain. While it was kitted with impressive software, there was something to be said for the Kyven touch, and parking and launching benefitted from both.

Once we were further out, I was relieved when the hub disappeared behind us and there weren't any other humans around us that might stare at me. It was a nice village, different in architecture from Kyven, but not in atmosphere. The people here seemed to remember Heather, even if it had been a while, and they were all asking why she was buying all these supplies, where she moved, what she was up to.

It worried me that they were a curious species, especially after I showed my true colours. I read weird things in the research about their obsession with finding life in outer space and stories about poking and prodding.

I'd never prodded anyone in my life.

The dashboard beeped and a warning flashed up.

"What's that?" Heather asked.

"Obstruction notice," I told her, peering out the

front window to see what the scanner might be picking up on. As far as I could tell, there was nothing out of the ordinary. Just green meadows with little stone walls, the occasional tree, and a winding road.

We turned the corner and a sea of moving white bushes came into view, spilling down from the hills and spreading all over the path and coming towards us.

"Rak!" I activated the emergency brake, bringing the shuttle to a halt just before we collided with the walking clouds. What was this?

19

HEATHER

I waved my arms to make myself bigger, hoping to stop the whole flock of sheep from trampling us and the van. They were lucky the guidance system had flagged their presence early or we might have crashed in them.

Standing by the van-shuttle, Atina had a worried and confused look on her face. "What are they?"

"Sheep. Haven't I shown you pictures before?"

She shook her head. "I don't think so. They look kind of like rashipis."

"They do, don't they? But aren't they much cuter?" I blocked the path of one trying to break free from the group. "And they're probably Farmer Jeffrey's. These are his meadows and his gates and fences are always breaking down. Everyone keeps telling him to repair them properly but he's a cheapskate."

"What's a cheapskate?" Atina asked.

"Someone who won't pay for things they need," I explained, peering out at the horizon to get an idea of how many sheep we were dealing with. It was hard to estimate but I guessed it looked near five hundred or so. Nearly twice as many as I was used to dealing with and that was with the help of a sheep dog or Rachel.

Atina patted the van. "We can just fly over them."

"I don't think that's wise," I told her, worried it might spook the herd and have them scatter. Besides the obvious panic it would cause for the animals, it would also draw attention to us if someone happened to come by and I was already paranoid that someone might be following us, some sketchy government type that wanted to lock us both up and experiment on Atina. I couldn't let that happen. No, we needed to get through the sheep without causing a scene.

There was only one solution.

"Let's see if we can herd the sheep back into their pastures," I said. "But we can't do this on our own. We need help."

"Does the help have to be real?" Atina asked thoughtfully.

"What are you thinking of?"

"I could create holographic copies of you. They won't work if you have to physically touch the animals, but it's about them seeing you, it might work."

"Wow, that's... I don't know what to say. Copies of me? Like clones?"

"Holographic copies," she emphasised. "Their

movements can be controlled by the shuttle's AI or manually by me. If you tell me where you want them to go and how to behave, we can even stay in here and don't have to get too close to the cloudlings."

"Cloudlings?" I laughed. "That's funny, one of my sheep back on Kyven is called that. And I suppose we can try it. They're already all over the road, so it won't do any harm. Although I would like to be outside with them. It's easier to get a feel for the mood of the flock when I can observe them up close."

I could see Atina wasn't comfortable with the thought of joining the flock. "You can stay inside and control my doubles from here. How will you know which one is the real me?"

She winked at me. "I couldn't mistake you even for your own clone."

Was that a compliment? I wasn't sure, so I simply smiled and put on my coat. I wasn't wearing the best shoes for herding sheep, but once we got back to the spaceship, the magic clothes cleaner there could get rid of all the mud I would most likely attract.

Atina did something on the shuttle controls. I didn't even try to understand what was flashing across the screens. She muttered something to herself while I mentally prepared myself for the task. I'd never dealt with such a huge flock at once. Hopefully, these holographic doppelgangers would make the job easier, or at least possible.

"Ready," the Kyven announced. I was glad she

looked like herself again with her vivid blue hair and skin. "They're waiting for you outside."

That sounded ominous. I took a deep breath and stepped out of the van-shuttle.

Even though I knew what awaited me, I still had to do a double take. It was like staring into ten mirrors at once, except that the images in the mirrors moved independently from me. Ten Heathers stood in a semi-circle around the van, wearing exactly the same things as me, their hair in the same loose ponytail as my own.

This had to be the craziest thing I'd ever seen in my life.

"Are you alright?" Atina asked from within the shuttle. "You're not moving."

"I just need a moment. This is freaky. Is this what I look like from the back? My neck is all weird."

"Your neck is perfect."

Okay, that was a compliment. Was she flirting with me? Even after I'd pushed her back? Not that I'd sent particularly clear signals by kissing her a second time. It had been a spur of the moment thing when I'd realised that she'd given up her own disguise just to save me an uncomfortable encounter with my neighbour who would ask way too many questions about my disappearance. It had been such a selfless thing that I'd reacted without thinking. Kissing her had been the first thing on my mind.

What did that say about my feelings for her? Those hadn't diminished at all, on the contrary, but what I'd told her earlier was still the truth. Our lives were so very different, which was becoming clearer with the second. She was working some crazy alien technology-slash-magic, while I was about to herd sheep. We weren't compatible in the long run. It was a nice holiday romance, but I doubted it could turn into more.

"Is something wrong?" Atina called.

"No, I'll start now! Can you make the doubles follow me closely and then spread out when I give the signal? I don't want the sheep to run before they're in the right position."

"I can do even better than that." A moment later, my doppelgangers were gone. "Just tell me when to turn them on again. I'll be able to hear you, the shuttle's mics are tuned into your sound waves."

Not being surrounded by ten holographic Heathers instantly made me feel better. I wasn't a vain person, on the contrary. I'd spent most of my life caked in mud rather than make up, so staring into a mirror wasn't something I did a lot.

I slowly walked towards the closest sheep, careful as not to spook it. Now that the herd had stopped moving, they were spread out across the road and the neighbouring meadows, quite a distance from the enclosure they were supposed to be in. This wasn't going to be easy.

My last herding job on Earth. That realisation caused my throat to tighten. Maybe it was for the best. One big, glorious goodbye to this life. When my cousin and I had left a year ago, everything had gone so fast that I'd barely had time to process what was happening.

This was what I'd needed, not visiting our old farm. One last time as a shepherd.

I stopped walking.

One last time. Was that it? The solution to it all? Instead of doing one last shepherding job on Earth, it would also be the last time overall? Was I ready to give it all up, not just on Earth, but on Kyven, too? I'd tried to continue living my life there as I had back home, but it clearly wasn't making me happy. I saw how much happier my cousin was. She'd found the life she wanted. I hadn't...yet.

"Should I start the holo generator?" Atina's voice was right in my ear, sounding as if she stood next to me.

"No, wait a moment... I need to think."

I knew that sounded silly, but this moment felt strangely profound. One of those moments that could change a life forever.

I looked at the herd of sheep all around me. I'd spent most of my life being surrounded by animals. I loved them. I'd thought I'd do this until I was too old to continue. But now things were different. My old dreams were no longer what I wanted, although it had taken me until now to realise that. Being a shepherd on my own little farm wasn't my only ambition any longer. I wanted more.

I wasn't quite sure exactly what more was but I knew it included Atina somehow. I just had to figure out how to make it happen without playing with her heart.

20

ATINA

Watching multiple versions of Heather on the path with a moving sea of white fluff was a bemusing and confusing sight. The sheep reminded me of rashipis with their dumb bleating and vacant stares, albeit a little cuter and fluffier. They seemed totally fooled by the holo projections of Heather and were happily trotting along.

It was a lovely sight and I could tell Heather was in her element, just like when we dealt with the rashipis. She was confident and calm, with slow movements and a commanding voice that would have even Captain Ellabee do her bidding.

It was easy enough to know which version of her was real, too. Besides her having that spark of life that the others missed, whenever one of the copies stood in the sunlight wrong, they slightly shimmered. A weird side effect that I hadn't expected. The sunlight must have different properties than the sun on Kyven.

Heather's voice came through the shuttle's audio feed. "Someone's coming, quick, turn the clones off."

I shut the holo generator off and the other versions of her vanished without a trace just in time as a group of humans came jogging around the corner with some barking four-footers. A male with silver hair and a leathery face raised his hand in a greeting. "Hey! You found my sheep!"

Heather waved back. "Hello, Jeff. Why am I not surprised that they got out again?"

Surprise bloomed on the man's face. "Heather, is that you? My goodness, it is. I thought you left the area. Well, where the devil have you come from?"

"You wouldn't believe it if I told you," Heather joked, looking at me and winking.

The older man shook her hand. "It's good to see you."

"Likewise. You should really get those gates repaired. They got all the way to Three Point Crossing already."

"Really? And you herded them all this way back already? Just on your lonesome?" another member of the group said.

Heather pointed at me. "I had a little help. We used the van to our advantage."

Not wanting to make any more blunders, I stayed safely put where I was. Besides, the sheep were kind of scary. There were so many of them and it was weird how they moved as a single organism.

"Well, we'll take it from here," the old man said, whistling on his fingers to jolt the others in action. "You should come back with us, we'll treat you to a nice hot meal."

"As lovely as that offer is, we have to get going, I'm afraid. Good luck with the sheep, Jeff." Heather came back to the van and climbed in next to me, a strange smile on her face.

"Everything okay?" I asked, trying to decipher her mood. She seemed elated and sat at the same time.

Heather gave me a small nod. "Yes, just... trying to work some things out. Jeff and his sons should be able to get the herd under control in no time, then we can get out of here."

"You're good at that." I gestured to the moving flock of cloudlings. "No wonder you did so well with the rashipis."

"Thanks. I've been herding sheep for as long as I can remember. It was Granny Elise who taught me but it was my mum who did it on the farm. She was amazing, always leading from the front with a gentle voice and a hand full of food. When they passed... I took her place and it's in those moments that I can feel her with me, in here." She gingerly touched her chest. "I could never give it up, there's no doubt about it, but it's only a part of me. There are so many other things I want to do in life, things I want to see. My bucket list was long when I still lived here, but now that I've seen how vast the universe is, there are infinitely more things I want to try. I'm just not sure how to combine those two."

I nodded quietly, better understanding now why she said before that we lived different lives or why it would be hard to be mated without either of us giving up our home. But where did that leave us?

Sensing there was more on her mind but that she wasn't ready to share it yet, I waited until the path was clear and set the shuttle in motion again. It would only be a short drive back to Leeds to pick up the other two passengers and then it was almost time for the PoTA-2 to depart. I had no doubt Captain Ellabee would put everyone non-essential in stasis again which meant I'd be all alone again.

I never minded that much on past flights but the idea of not getting to enjoy Heather's company made my gut clench uncomfortably. Once we arrived on Kyven, she would go back to her farm and I already had another job with Captain Ellabee lined up that would take me galaxies away from her.

My hands tightened in my lap as the shuttle continued along its route on autopilot. I desperately wanted a solution for how we could stay together but it was time to face reality, the adventure was almost over and I'd have to say goodbye soon.

We got back to the PoTA-2 far too quickly. Most of the crew were on shore leave and Sahra and Abby were still with the human's parents, but Captain Ellabee sat on the bridge. I didn't think she ever took a break. In all the time I'd worked on the ship, Ellabee had never taken a single holiday. She only ever left the PoTA-2 to meet with suppliers and clients, but not for pleasure.

"Atina, I'm glad you're back!" she said as soon as she saw us enter. "I've been plotting our route and could do with a second opinion."

I shot an apologetic glance at Heather, but she just smiled at me. "I'll leave you to it. I could really do with a shower after all that shepherding."

I watched her walk away, her hips swaying. She really was one of the prettiest females I'd ever seen. Pretty, talented, clever, generous, funny... Oh my, I really had fallen ears over toes for her. And I realised that no matter our differences, I couldn't let her go.

"Captain, there's something I'd like to discuss with you first."

"Yes?" Ellabee gave me a sharp look, her full attention on me. That's why she was the captain. She knew how to both inspire and intimidate her crew.

"I've been thinking..."

"Don't you dare say you're going to quit because you've fallen in love," the captain interrupted me. "You're my best pilot. I refuse to lose you."

I was surprised she was being this frank. And how did she even know?

"Come on, it's obvious. You've got the look of a lovesick squiidi. Anyone with at least one eye will have seen it."

My ears throbbed with embarrassment. I didn't like being compared to the feathered mammal that was known for imprinting on their mate with such passion that they never spend another minute apart. Although now that I'd met Heather, I understood the squiidi's desire to be with their mates a little better.

"I..."

I didn't know what to say. Luckily, Ellabee interrupted me yet again.

"I did some thinking while you were gone. I was certain it would come to this, so I wanted to be prepared. As I said, you're the best pilot I've ever had. Katak is good, but you have that edge that I want in my crew. How about this: I will give your mate a job on my ship and you two can share a cabin. After the incident with the escaped rashipis, I've been wondering whether it might be worth employing someone to look after any live cargo we transport. Heather might be just the right person for the job. What do you say?"

"I'd have to talk to Heather," I hedged to cover my surprise. This would be the perfect solution to how we could combine our two very different lives.

The captain mistook my hesitation for wanting to bargain. "Alright, what do you want? A raise? Extra shore leave?"

If she offered...

"I would like Heather to be paid the same wage as me. And when we return to Kyven, a month of shore leave so I can visit Heather's animal park and meet her family."

"Deal." The ease with which Ellabee agreed made me think that I could have gone for a lot more. I'd have to keep that in mind. As much as I was happy with my current salary, it could always be a little more.

"Two months?" I tried, but it was too late.

"Don't test your luck," the captain grinned. "Now help me plot this route. Prove to me that I've made the right decision."

[21]

HEATHER

The purple-blue grass around the spaceport that had once looked alien to me now welcomed me home.

Next to me, Atina breathed in deeply. "Kyven air. It's sweeter than that on Earth. I feel like every planet has its own distinct smell."

She was right. Not that I had more than two planets to compare, and I wasn't sure I'd ever step foot on another one.

Behind us, Abby and Sahra disembarked, hand in hand, chatting happily. We'd only woken up from stasis about an hour ago, but those two looked a lot more awake than I felt. I'd not had much time to talk to them, nor to Atina. Captain Ellabee had kept her pilots busy ever since we'd returned to the ship. I'd kind of wondered if the captain knew what had happened at the cafe and was now punishing Atina for it. At least I'd had Jiji for company before we'd all been put into stasis. The pink ball of fluff sat on Atina's shoulder, chirping happily. I reached out and tickled what I thought was its chin. It squiggled with delight. So cute.

My controlband vibrated. A message from my cousin popped up, informing me that she was going to be there in a few minutes to pick us up. While I was looking forward to seeing her, I'd hoped for a moment longer with Atina before we had to part ways.

Someone had already unloaded my luggage and Sahra and Abby had helpfully offered to take the bench in their shuttle. Somehow, the whole adventure was almost over and I didn't quite know how it had happened. No, I did know. Stasis. It had robbed me from spending more time with the lovely pilot.

I stood in the port, my hands deep in the pockets of my jacket. I desperately wanted to reach out to Atina and pull her in a hug or even a kiss, but I didn't want to confuse us even more. "I guess this is it."

She looked at me with her sparkling green eyes. "It doesn't have to be. I didn't have the chance to talk to you before the captain put everyone in stasis, but she wants to offer you a job."

I wasn't sure if I heard her correctly. "Me? A job? On the ship? What would I do on a ship?"

"Look after live cargo. The rashipis were fine because they weren't in stasis super long this time but it's not ideal. We delivered them on the way back but the supplier didn't pay his full fee because of that. It was still worth it though, live animal transportation is a lucrative business and if there's something Captain Ellabee likes, it's riches. But if you stay on board, you and I could be together," Atina explained, looking so hopeful, it ached.

"Atina..." I took a step forward and took her hands in mine. Her six fingers fitted surprisingly perfect with mine and that was making what I had to say next all the harder. "As interesting as that sounds and as much as I'd love to spend more time with you, I can't just abandon the farm, or my cousin, to go off on wild adventures with you. I don't even know enough about rashipis or other animals you might transport. I'm not a keeper, I'm a shepherd."

A deep sadness filled her eyes. "You're not saying yes."

"I'm sorry. I wish I could, but I have duties, responsibilities, family I can't leave behind."

She nodded slowly. "I understand."

My controlband chimed again, notifying me Rachel had arrived with an alert that she was parked in a temporary spot.

"My cousin is here," I said, unmoving. I knew I had to go, that it was time to say goodbye, but I didn't want to. "When are you leaving?"

"We're setting off right away. I was going to take some shore leave if you accepted the job so I could spend some time with you here, but maybe it's better if I don't," Atina said.

I selfishly wanted her to do it anyway but I couldn't

ask that of her. Long distance relationships were hard enough on Earth; it was a whole other thing when she was zipping through space and was gone for who knew how long. It just wouldn't work.

My voice came out shaky. "When will you be back?"

"Our next trip is taking us to Port Amitin, it's three milky ways from here so we probably won't be back before the national holiday."

"That's a long time," I said, my stomach already twisting into tight knots that I wouldn't get to see her for this long. "Are you going to be okay?"

Atina took a small step forward, her smile not quite reaching her eyes. "Of course, I'm made of good stuff."

My band chirped again, twice, harshly.

"I'll let you go," Atina said. "Just know that I loved having you on the ship."

I rested my forehead against hers. "I loved it too. I'm sorry that I have to stay."

She chuckled softly. "I'll think of you when I'm among the stars. Goodbye, Heather." She turned and walked back up to the ship, her green hair dancing in the sweet Kyven wind.

I couldn't believe I was letting her go. With every step, my stomach twisted and churned more but I kept going. I couldn't shake the feeling that I was making a terrible mistake but what other choice did I have? I belonged on my farm. Well, the cottage... It wasn't really a farm anymore, or mine.

In the shuttle bay, I spotted Rachel waiting for me.

"Heather!" She waved enthusiastically and ran to me, practically throwing herself in my arms. "You're back!"

I tightened my arms around her and some of the pain dulled. Not all of it, but some. "Missed me?"

"Loads. I think this is the longest we've been apart since we were like... I don't know, seventeen."

I chuckled. "Yeah, it's weird when we're apart, isn't it?"

Rachel nodded as she pulled me to the shuttle. She'd got one where we could sit upright instead of having to lie down. "So how was your trip? Tell me *everything*. Did you like the spaceship? How was Earth? Did you visit the farm? What was it like?"

"Woah, slow down, slow down. What's the rush? I'm back now so we have all the time in the world to talk," I noted bitterly. Luckily, Rachel didn't notice.

"It's just good to see you. I have something to tell you and I'm not sure how you're going to feel about it. So some of the sheep escaped but don't worry, we got them back. But the situation sparked a conversation with Tamsia and I kind of adopted a hundag. It's sort of like a sheepdog but it can fly so it's even better at herding. I know I should've run it past you first but I saw his fluffy face and fell in love instantly."

I chuckled, not in the slightest surprised. Rachel always had a tendency of bringing strays home. "We did need a sheepdog."

"That's what I thought. He's green so I named him Kiwi. Timothy already loves teasing him," she babbled. "It's been hectic while you've been gone. Tamsia has been helping out a lot and she's actually really good with the animals. It's funny because she says she never really liked the Kyven creatures in their animal park but she likes ours."

"I'm glad to hear that." I did my best to smile, not wanting to infect her with my mood. As good as it was to see her again and hear about the state of things, I couldn't stop thinking about the spaceship leaving and Atina with it.

Rachel frowned and looked at me, the advantages of autopilot. "Everything okay?"

"Yes, everything's great. I'm glad to be..." I hesitated. Home didn't sound right. "Back."

"Tell your face that. Is something the matter? Did you not have fun in space? Or on Earth?"

Part of me wanted to tell her everything but I didn't want her to think I was going to abandon her. She was the only family I had left and we needed to stick together.

I offered her the most convincing smile I could muster. "It was lovely."

"Hmm..." Rachel studied me thoroughly. "I don't buy it. You have the same expression on your face as that time we purchased Hamish even though we technically didn't have enough money for a new bull but you went ahead with it anyway because I really wanted him. What are you not telling me? Do you want to move back to Earth?"

"No, that's not it."

"Aha, but there is something!" Rachel exclaimed triumphantly. "Come on, out with it."

"I met someone. Her name is Atina, she's a pilot on the PoTA-2. But she loves her job and is about to set off for another milky way. Her captain did offer me a job to look after live cargo but I have the animals and I don't want to leave you. So I'm just a little sad but I'll get over it," I said, wanting to make it clear that I wasn't going anywhere.

Rachel was quiet for a moment. "Are you in love?"

"I think... No, I *know* I have feelings for her. But it doesn't matter, I belong here."

My cousin laughed softly. "Look around, Heather. The whole planet is purple, the people are blue, neither of us belong here. We uprooted our whole life to be here because *I* fell in love."

"Well, and because the bank was going to take our farm and our animals."

"Yes, that too. But you didn't have to come with me."

"I didn't want to say goodbye to you," I told her, taking her hand in mine.

A smile brightened Rachel's face. "And we're not saying goodbye, you idiot. But we don't have to be attached by the hip either. If you want to stretch your wings, you can. It's about time you flew the nest."

"What about the farm? The animals? I can't just leave all the sheep and cows and chickens behind to travel around space."

"Then don't. Ever heard of part-time jobs? And

now that Tamsia is going to do more around the farm and that we have Kiwi to help with herding the sheep, you won't have to do as much. How about this: After the lambing season, you join your woman for a few months? That gives you enough time to get everything in order and maybe even train an assistant. Then you can work on the ship with her for another few months."

My cousin made it sound easy. And maybe it was. I threw my arms around Rachel and embraced her tighter than ever. "I love you, you're the best."

"Does this mean I'm turning the shuttle around?" she asked.

"Turn it around! I have a ship to catch!"

ATINA

I didn't take notice of anything until I was back in my cabin and the door closed behind me. I felt like curling up into a ball and drown in self-pity.

Heather was gone. She'd chosen a life without me. I'd likely never see her again. She'd be on Kyven with her fluffy white cloud-animals while I was travelling the stars, so very far away. My belly felt wrong, as if something was missing. It hurt worse than after a disembowelment. My bowels always grew back, but I wasn't sure if this invisible wound would ever heal.

Still, it was good to know that Heather was safe and well. I didn't want her to be unhappy just to be with me. I wasn't that selfish, no matter how much it hurt to be apart from her.

I looked around my cabin. It looked so very empty. So boring. I realised I didn't even have a picture of

Heather. Maybe that was for the best. I should try and forget about her as fast as possible before I went crazy. I had to focus on my job. Not concentrating during a launch or landing could mean certain death not just for me, but for the entire crew of the PoTA-2.

My controlband vibrated. Captain Ellabee wanted to see me on the bridge. I didn't look forward to telling her that she was going to have to look for someone else to care for live cargo, but at least this would distract me from my grief.

I ignored the crew members I saw on the way to the bridge, heading there as fast as I could. I didn't feel like talking to anyone. To be honest, I didn't feel like doing anything at all. What I wanted was Heather, but I couldn't have her.

Ellabee was alone on the bridge. I was glad. Katak had the emotional intelligence of a rashipi and I didn't feel like explaining to him why I felt the way I did.

The captain didn't ask me what had happened or whether Heather was going to join her crew. Instead, she pointed at the door that led to my cockpit.

"I need you to unlock your station for your replacement. I can't be bothered to look for the access codes in the manual."

Replacement? My hearts sank. Was she firing me?

"What have I done wrong?" I asked, my voice quivering.

"Wrong? Nothing. Unless you count falling in love as a mistake."

Rak. Maybe she thought that I wouldn't be able to focus on my job without Heather.

Ellabee got up from her captain's chair and headed towards my cockpit. "Come on, let's do this. You don't want to keep her waiting."

"What?"

She smirked, clearly enjoying my confusion. "Heather is waiting for you in the spaceport terminal. All you have to do is unlock your work station and pack your things, then your shore leave can begin."

"But..."

"As much as I like seeing you speechless, I have other things to do today. Hurry up."

"But Heather... She..."

"She called me to let me know that she'd accept the job as long as she gets to take regular leaves of absences to return to her farm. Something about needing to help her animals have baby animals. I didn't want to know the details of how that's done. Obviously, you won't get as much leave as she will. I can schedule our cargo runs around whether we have her to look after live animals, but I can't fly without a pilot. This month of shore leave is an exception. And I'm happy to shorten it to a week if you don't unlock your console this very moment."

My hands shook slightly as I keyed in my passwords to authorise others to use my cockpit station. As much as I tried to stay calm and professional on the outside, inside my thoughts were racing. Heather had come back. She was waiting for me. She was going to work on this very ship. We'd be together. This wasn't the end after all.

I finished the job as fast as I possibly could, then hurried away as soon as Ellabee was satisfied that my temporary replacement would be able to log into the console. There were always a bunch of pilots hanging about spaceports waiting to be hired in cases like this, so I was sure the captain would find a partner for Katak quickly.

I was already on the way to the airlock when I realised I had to get my things. I ran to my cabin, threw a few clothes into a bag while Jiji released curious chirps. I put my beloved companion on my shoulder and rushed back towards the exit. I didn't want to keep Heather waiting for any longer than necessary. What if she changed her mind? I couldn't let that happen.

The ship suddenly felt a lot bigger than before. Had the corridor to the airlock always been this long? By the time I finally stepped onto solid ground and passed through the security gates, my hearts seemed to burst out of my chest with worry and excitement. But there she was, sitting on a bench in the main terminal, standing out among all the Kyvens not just because she was alien, but also because she was mine. My mate. At least, I hoped that this is what it meant.

I stood there for a moment, dumbfounded and afraid to approach her in case it would break the spell.

Jiji squealed in excitement, bouncing up and down my shoulder and drawing Heather's attention. Her eyes brightened and pink blushes bloomed on her cheeks like the sun rising on Kyven and my hearts swelled looking at her. She was a vision and I couldn't believe she was here.

The beautiful human jogged towards me, slightly panting as she paused in front of me. "Hey."

"You came back," I whispered, breathless in her place. "I don't understand, I thought you couldn't leave your animals, your cousin. I thought... that you didn't want me."

Heather captured me in a mouth kiss that made my ears tingle and glow so hot, they might as well have caught fire. I embraced her as wholly and fully as I could, still not believing that she was really here.

"Of course, I want you," Heather said when she pulled back, her cheeks even redder and her eyes slightly darkened. "That was never the problem. It was my old life."

"What changed?"

"I spoke to Rachel and she was... fine. She missed me and she was glad to see me, but she doesn't need me. Or rather, not all the time. I'll still be needed for lambing and calving season but her mate has stepped up while I was gone and we'll look for someone to help out as well." Heather spoke so fast, I was worried she wasn't breathing. "But driving away made me realise how much I wanted to stay. If it's not too late."

I shook my head. "I never blamed or resented you for staying. I actually admire you for having somewhere to return to. I wish I had that."

She laced her fingers through mine. "Now you have me."

"And you're sure?"

"Yes." She looked up at me, her arms still warm around me. "Atina, I have a really important question to ask you."

"Okay?"

"Will you be my mate?"

I didn't have to think twice. My hearts virtually beat out of my chest and I could only nod, tears welling up in my eyes.

"I accept." I gently tickled Heather's ear, running my finger along the rounded shell, a gesture only meant for the most important person in one's life.

Heather kissed me again, softer and sweeter.

Jiji chirped in protest and we broke apart, laughing.

"I can't wait to introduce you to my cousin and show you all our animals," Heather murmured, reaching up to tickle the demanding qoark. "You're going to love it, both of you. Especially Timo. I bet he and Jiji will get on."

"We'll see about that," I said, not entirely convinced. Her earth animals were weird but I looked forward to figuring them out.

"I'm sure you will." She took my hands in hers? "Shall we go home, then?"

Emotion overwhelmed me and I could only nod. All these journeys and adventures through the stars searching for somewhere to belong and finally I found it, standing right in front of me with the most beautiful adoring smile I'd ever seen.

I was already home.

Thank you for reading The Alien's Shepherd. We hope you enjoyed reading about how Heather found her own Kyven romance with the lovely pilot Atina. If you're loving the fun mix of aliens and animals, make sure you read The Alien's Reindeer for a holiday special, more accidental abduction, and more quirky animals.

If you're in the mood for more aliens and sci-fi romance, take a look at Skye's books:
skyemackinnon.com/scifi
And if you want more f/f romance, check out Arizona's books: arizonatape.com

Don't want to miss a new release? Subscribe to our newsletters:
skyemackinnon.com/newsletter
arizonatape.com/subscribe

ALIENS AND ANIMALS

1. The Alien's Zookeeper - Bavalla and Tilly

2. The Alien's Veterinarian - Sahra and Abby

3. The Alien's Farmer - Tamsia and Rachel

4. The Alien's Shepherd - Heather and Atina

5. The Alien's Reindeer

skyemackinnon.com/aliensandanimals

ABOUT SKYE MACKINNON

Skye MacKinnon is a USA Today & International Bestselling Author whose books are filled with strong heroines who don't have to choose.

She embraces her Scottishness with fantastical Scottish settings and a dash of mythology, no matter if she's writing about aliens in kilts, Celtic gods, cat shifters, or the streets of Edinburgh.

When she's not typing away at her favourite cafe, Skye loves dried mango, as much exotic tea as she can squeeze into her cupboards, and being covered in pet hair by her hyperactive kitten.

Subscribe to her newsletter:
skyemackinnon.com/newsletter

Join her Facebook Reader Group:
facebook.com/groups/skyesbookharem

facebook.com/skyemackinnonauthor

twitter.com/skye_mackinnon

instagram.com/skyemackinnonauthor

bookbub.com/authors/skye-mackinnon

goodreads.com/SkyeMacKinnon

tiktok.com/@skyemackinnonauthor

Arizona Tape lives her dream life hanging out with her dog and writing stories all day.

Her favourite books to write are urban fantasy and paranormal romances with queer leads, stories that she wished were around when she was younger.

When she's not writing, she can be found cooking up a storm in the kitchen, watching shows that make her cry, or trying her hand at her new hobby of the week.

She currently lives in the United Kingdom with her girlfriend and her adorable dog who is the star of her newsletter.

Sign up here for adorable pictures, free books, and news about her books: www.arizonatape.com/subscribe

FOLLOW ARIZONA TAPE

- Website: www.arizonatape.com
- Mailing List: www.arizonatape.com/subscribe

- Reader Group: http://facebook.com/
  groups/arizonatape

www.ingramcontent.com/pod-product-compliance
Lightning Source LLC
Chambersburg PA
CBHW021438150726
47989CB00001B/296